THE MELTING OF MOLLY

Melted

THE
MELTING OF MOLLY

By
MARIA THOMPSON DAVIESS

Author of
Miss Selina Lue, The Road to Providence,
Rose of Old Harpeth, Etc., Etc.

ILLUSTRATED BY
R. M. CROSBY

INDIANAPOLIS
THE BOBBS-MERRILL COMPANY
PUBLISHERS

PRESS OF
BRAUNWORTH & CO.
BOOKBINDERS AND PRINTERS
BROOKLYN, N. Y.

LEAVES FROM
THE BOOK OF MOLLY

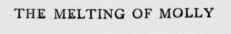

THE MELTING OF MOLLY

The Melting of Molly

LEAF FIRST

THE BACHELOR'S-BUTTONS

YES, I truly think that in all the world there is nothing so dead as a young widow's deceased husband, and God ought to give His wisest man-angel special charge concerning looking after her and the devil at the same time. They both need it! I don't know how all this is going to end and I wish my mind wasn't in a kind of tingle. However, I'll do the best I can and not hold myself at all responsible for myself, and then who will there be to blame?

There are a great many kinds of good=

feeling in this world, from radiant joy down to perfect bliss, but this spring I have got an attack of just old-fashioned happiness that looks as if it might become chronic.

I am so happy that I planted my garden all crooked, my eyes upon the clouds with the birds sailing against them, and when I became conscious I found wicked flaunting poppies sprouted right up against the sweet modest clover-pinks, while the whole paper of bachelor's-buttons was sowed over everything—which I immediately began to dig right up again, blushing furiously to myself over the trowel, and glad that I had caught myself before they grew up to laugh in my face. However, I got that laugh anyway, and I might just as well have left them, for Billy ran to the gate and called Doctor John to come in and make Molly stop digging up his buttons. Billy claims everything in this garden, and he thought they would grow up into the kind of buttons you pop out of a gun.

"So you're digging up the bachelor-pops, Mrs. Molly?" the doctor asked as he leaned over the gate. I went right on digging without looking up at him. I couldn't look up because I was blushing still worse. Sometimes I hate that man, and if he wasn't Billy's father I wouldn't neighbor with him as I do. But somebody *has* to look after Billy.

I believe it will be a real relief to write down how I feel about him in his old book and I shall do it whenever I can't stand him any longer, and if he gave the horrid, red leather thing to me to make me miserable, he can't do it; not this spring! I wish I dared burn it up and forget about it, but I don't! This record on the first page is enough to *reduce* me—to tears, and I wonder why it doesn't.

I weigh one hundred and sixty pounds, down in black and white, and it is a tragedy! I don't believe that man at the grocery store is so very reliable in his weights, though he had a very pleasant smile while he was weighing me. Still I had better get some scales of my own, smiles are so deceptive.

I am five feet three inches tall or short, whichever way one looks at me. I thought I was taller, but I suppose I will have to believe my own yardstick.

But as to my waist measure, I positively refuse to write that down, even if I have promised Doctor John a dozen times over to do it, while I only really left him to *suppose* I would. It is bad enough to know that your belt has to be reduced to twenty-three inches without putting down

4

how much it measures now in figures to insult yourself with. No, I intend to have this for my happy spring.

Yes, I suppose it would have been lots better for my happiness if I had kept quiet about it all, but at the time I thought I had to advise with him over the matter. Now I'm sorry I did. That is one thing about being a widow, you are accustomed to advising with a man, whether you want to or not, and you can't get over the habit right away. Poor Mr. Carter hasn't been dead much over a year and I must be missing him most awfully, though just lately I can't remember not to forget about him a great deal of the time. Now if he had been here—*horrors!*

Still, that letter was enough to upset anybody, and no wonder I ran right across my garden, through Billy's hedge-hole and over into Doctor John's office to tell him about it; but I ought not to have been agitated enough to let him take the letter right out of my hand and read it.

"So after ten years Al Bennett is coming back to pop his bachelor's-buttons at you, Mrs. Molly?" he said in the deep drawling voice he always uses when he makes fun of Billy and me and which never fails to make us both mad. I didn't look at him directly, but I felt his hand shake with the letter in it.

"Not ten, only *eight!* He went when I was seventeen," I answered with dignity, wishing I dared be snappy at him; though I never am.

"And after eight years he wants to come back and find you squeezed into a twenty-inch-waist, blue muslin rag you wore at parting? No wonder Al didn't succeed at bank clerking, but had to make his hit at diplomacy and the high arts.

Some hit at that to be legationed at Saint James! He's such a big gun that it is a pity he had to return to his native heath and find even such a slight disappointment as a one-yard waist measure around his— his—"

"Oh it's not, it's *not* that much." I fairly gasped and I couldn't help the tears coming into my eyes. I have never said much about it, but nobody knows how it hurts me to be all this fat! Just writing it down in a book mortifies me dreadfully. It's been coming on worse and worse every year since I married. Poor Mr. Carter had a very good appetite and I don't know why I should have felt that I had to eat so much every day to keep him company; I wasn't always so considerate of him. Then he didn't want me to dance any more because married women oughtn't, or ride horseback either—no amusement left but himself and weekly prayer-meetings, and — and — I just couldn't help the tears coming and dripping as I thought about it all and that awful waist measure in inches.

"Stop crying this minute, Molly," said Doctor John suddenly in the deep voice he uses to Billy and me when we are really sick or stump-toed. "You know I was only teasing you and I won't stand for—"

But I sobbed some more. I like him when his eyes come out from under his bushy brows and are all tender and full of sorry for us.

"I can't help it," I gulped in my sleeve. "I did used to like Alfred Bennett. My heart almost broke when he went away. I used to be beautiful and slim, and now I feel as if my own fat ghost has come to haunt me all my life. I am so ashamed! If a woman can't cry over her own dead

8

"Will you do just as I tell you?"

beauty, what can she cry over?" By this time I was really crying.

Then what happened to me was that Doctor John took me by the shoulders and gave me one good shake and then made me look him right in the eyes through the tears and all.

"You foolish child," he said in the deepest voice I almost ever heard him use. "You are just a lovely, round, luscious peach, but if you will be happier to have Al Bennett come and find you as slim as a string-bean I can show you how to do it. Will you do just as I tell you?"

"Yes, I will," I sniffed in a comforted voice. What woman wouldn't be comforted by being called a "luscious peach". I looked out between my fingers to see what more he was going to say, but he had turned to a shelf and taken down two books.

9

"Now," he said in his most business-like voice, as cool as a bucket of water fresh from the spring, "it is no trouble at all to take off your surplus avoirdupois at the rate of two and a half pounds a week if you follow these directions. As I take it you are about twenty-five pounds over your normal weight. It will take over two months to reduce you and we will allow an extra month for further beautifying, so that when Mr. Bennett arrives he will find the lady of his adoration in proper trim to be adored. Yes, just be still until I copy these directions in this little, red leather blank-book for you, and every day I want you to keep an exact record of the conditions of which I make note. No, don't talk while I make out these diet lists! I wish you would go across the hall and see if you don't think we ought to get Bill a thinner set of night-drawers. It seems to me he must be too warm in the ones he is wearing."

When he speaks to me in that tone of voice I always do it. And I needed Billy badly at that very moment. I took him out of his little cot by Doctor John's big bed and sat down with him in my arms over by the window through which the early moon came streaming. Billy is so little, little not to have a mother to rock him all the times he needs it that I take every opportunity to give it to him I find —when he's unconscious and can't help himself. She died before she ever even saw him and I've always tried to do what I could to make it up to him.

Poor Mr. Carter said when Billy cut his teeth that a neighbor's baby can be worse than twins of your own. He didn't like children and the baby's crying disturbed him, so many a night I walked

Billy out in the garden until daylight, while Mr. Carter and Doctor John both slept. Always his little, warm, wilty body has comforted me for the emptiness of not having a baby of my own. And he's very congenial, too, for he's slim and flowery, pink and dimply, and as mannish as his father, in funny little flashes.

"Git a stick to punch it, Molly," he was murmuring in his sleep. Then I heard the doctor call me and I had to kiss him, put him back in his bed, and go across the hall.

Doctor John was standing by the table with this horrid small book in his hand and his mouth was set in a straight line and his eyes were deep back under their brows. I hate him that way, too, and I would like to get up so close to him that he couldn't *hit* me or have a door locked between us. It's strange how the thought of taking a beating from a man can make a woman's heart jump. Mine jumped so it was hard to look as meek as I felt best under the circumstances; but I looked it out from under my lashes cautiously.

"There you are, Mrs. Molly," he said briskly as he handed me this book. "Get weighed and measured and sized-up generally in the morning and follow all the directions. Also make every record I have noted so that I can have the proper data to help you as you go along—or rather down. And if you will be faithful about it to me, or rather Al, I think we can be sure of buttoning that blue muslin dress without even the aid of the button-hook." His voice had the "if you can" note in it that always sets me off.

"Had we better get the kiddie some thinner night-rigging?" he hastened to ask as I was just about to explode. He knows the signs.

"Thank you, Doctor Moore! I hate the very ground you walk on and I'll attend to those night-clothes myself to-morrow," I answered, and I sailed out of that office and down the path toward my own house beyond his hedge. But I carried this book tight in my hand and I made up my mind that I would do it all if it killed me. I would show him I could be *faithful*—to whom I would decide later on. But I hadn't read far into this book when I committed myself to myself like that!

I don't know just how long I sat on the front steps all by myself bathed in a perfect flood of moonlight and loneliness. It was not a bit of comfort to hear Aunt Adeline snoring away in her room down the dark hall. It takes the greatest congeniality to make a person's snoring a pleasure to anybody and Aunt Adeline and I are not that way.

THE BACHELOR'S-BUTTONS

When poor Mr. Carter died, the next day she said: "Now, Mary, you are entirely too young to live all your long years of widowhood alone, and as I am in the same condition, I will rent my cottage and move right up the street into your house to protect and console you." And she did, —the moving and the protecting.

Mr. Henderson has been dead forty-two years. He only lived three months after he married Aunt Adeline and her crêpe veil is over a yard long yet. Men are the dust under her feet, but she likes for Doctor John to come over and sit on the porch with us because she can consult with him about what Mr. Henderson really died of and talk with him about the sad state of poor Mr. Carter's liver for a year before he died. I just go on rocking Billy and singing hymns to him in such a way that I can't hear the conversation.

Mr. Carter's liver got on my nerves alive, and dead it does worse. But it hurts when the doctor has to take the little sleep-boy out of my arms to carry him home; though I like it when he says under his breath, "Thank you, Molly."

And as I sat and thought how near he and I had been to each other in all our troubles, I excused myself for running to him with that letter and I acknowledged to myself that I had no right to get mad when he teased me, for he had been kind and interested about helping me get thin by the time Alfred came back to see me. I couldn't tell which I was blushing all to myself about, the "luscious peach" he had called me or the "lovely lily" Alfred had reminded me in his letter that I had been when he left me.

Why don't people realize that a seventeen-year-old girl's heart is a sensitive wind-flower that may be shattered by a breath? Mine shattered when Alfred went away to find something he could do to make a living, and Aunt Adeline gave the hard green stem to Mr. Carter when she married me to him. Poor Mr. Carter!

No, I wasn't twenty, and this town was full of women who were aunts and cousins and law-kin to me, and nobody did anything for me. They all said with a sigh of relief, "It will be such a nice safe thing for you, Molly." And they really didn't mean anything by tying up a gay, dancing, frolicking, prancing colt of a girl with a terribly ponderous bridle. But God didn't want to see me always trotting along slow and tired and not caring what happened to me, even pounds and pounds of plumpness, so he found use for Mr. Carter in some other place but this world, and I feel that He is going to see me

through whatever happens. If some of
the women in my missionary society knew
how friendly I feel with God they would
put me out for contempt of court.

No, the town didn't mean anything by
chastening my spirit with Mr. Carter and
they didn't consider him in the matter at
all, poor man. Of that I feel sure. Hillsboro is like that. It settled itself here in
a Tennessee valley a few hundreds of
years ago and has been hatching and
clucking over its own small affairs ever
since. All the houses set back from the
street with their wings spread out over
their gardens, and mothers here go on
hovering even to the third and fourth gen-
eration. Lots of times young, long-leg-
ged, frying-size boys scramble out of the
nests and go off to college and decide to
grow up where their crow will be heard by
the world. Alfred was one of them.

THE BACHELOR'S-BUTTONS

And, too, occasionally some man comes along from the big world and marries a plump little broiler and takes her away with him, but mostly they stay and go to hovering life on a corner of the family estate. That's what I did.

I was a poor, little, lost chick with frivolous tendencies and they all clucked me over into this empty Carter nest which they considered well-feathered for me. It gave them all a sensation when they found out from the will just how well it was feathered. And it gave me one, too. All that money would make me nervous if Mr. Carter hadn't made Doctor John its guardian, though I sometimes feel that the responsibility of me makes him treat me as if he were my step-grandfather-in-law. But all in all, though stiff in its knees with aristocracy, Hillsboro is lovely and loving; and couldn't inquisitiveness be called just real affection with a kind of squint in its eye?

And there I sat on my front steps, being embraced in a perfume of everybody's lilacs and peachblow and sweet syringa and affectionate interest and moonlight, with a letter in my hand from the man whose two photographs and many letters I had kept locked up in the garret for years. Is it any wonder I tingled when he told me that he had never come back because he couldn't have me and that now the minute he landed in America he was going to lay his heart at my feet? I added his honors to his prostrate heart myself and my own beat at the prospect. All the eight years faded away and I was again back in the old garden down at Aunt Adeline's cottage saying good-by, folded up in his arms. That's the way my memory put the scene to me, but the word "folded" made me remember that blue muslin dress again. I had promised to keep it and wear it for him when he came back—and I couldn't forget that the blue belt was just twenty-three inches and mine is—no, I *won't* write it. I had got that dress out of the old trunk not ten minutes after I had read the letter and measured it.

No, nobody would blame me for running right across the garden to Doctor John with such a real trouble as that! All of a sudden I hugged the letter and the little book up close to my breast and laughed until the tears ran down my cheeks.

Then before I went into the house I assembled my garden and had family prayers with my flowers. I do that because they are all the family I've got, and God knows that all His budding things need encouragement, whether it is a widow or a snowball-bush. He'll give it to us!

And I'm praying again as I sit here and watch for the doctor's light to go out. I hate to go to sleep and leave it burning, for he sits up so late and he is so gaunt and thin and tired-looking most times. That's what the last prayer is about, almost always,—sleep for him and no night call!

LEAF SECOND

THE very worst page in this red— red devil—I'm glad I've written it at last—of a book is the fifth. It says:

"Breakfast—one slice of dry toast, one egg, fruit and a tablespoonful of baked cereal, small cup of coffee, no sugar, no cream." And me with two Jersey cows full of the richest cream in Hillsboro, Harpeth Valley, out in my pasture!

"Dinner, one small lean chop, slice of toast, spinach, green beans and lettuce salad. No dessert or sweet." The blue-grass in my yard is full of fat little fryers and I wish I were a sheep if I have to eat lettuce and spinach for grass. At least

I'd have more than one chop inside me then.

"Supper—slice of toast and an apple." Why the apple? Why supper at all?

Oh, I'm hungry, hungry until I cry in my sleep when I dream about a muffin! I thought at first that getting out of bed before my eyes are fairly open and turning myself into a circus actor by doing every kind of overhand, foot, arm and leg contortion that the mind of cruel man could invent to torture a human being with, would kill me before I had been at it a week, but when I read on page sixteen that as soon as all that horror was over I must jump right into the tub of cold water, I kicked, metaphorically speaking. And I've been kicking ever since, literally to keep from freezing.

But as cruel a death as freezing is, it doesn't compare to the tortures of being

She shrouds me for the agony

melted. Judy administers it to me and her faithful heart is so wrung with compassion that she perspires almost as much as I do. She wrings a linen sheet out in a caldron of boiling water and shrouds me in it for the agony—and then more and more blanket windings envelop me until I am like the mummy of some Egyptian giantess. I have ice on the back of my neck and my forehead, and murder for the whole world in my heart. Once I got so discouraged at the idea of having all this hades in this life that I mingled tears with the beads of perspiration that rolled down my cheeks, and she snatched me out of those steaming grave-clothes in less time than it takes to tell it, soused me in a tub of cold water, fed me a chicken wing and a hot biscuit and the information that I was "good-looking enough for *anybody* to eat up alive without all this foolishness," all in a very few seconds. Now I have to beg her to help me and I heard her tell her nephew, who does the gardening, that she felt like an undertaker with such goings-on. At any rate, if it all kills me it won't be my fault if anybody has to lie in saying that I was "beautiful in death".

But now that more than a month has passed, I really don't mind it so much. I feel so good and strong and prancy all the time that I can't keep from bubbling. I have to smile at myself.

Then another thing that helps is Billy and his ball. I never could really play with him before, but now I can't help it. But an awful thing happened about that yesterday. We were in the garden playing over by the lilac bushes and Billy always beats me because when he runs to base he throws himself down and slides

along on the grass on his little stomach
as he sees the real players do over at the
ball grounds. Then all of a sudden, before I knew it, I just did the same thing,
and we slid to the flower pot we use as a
base together, each on his own stomach.
And what did Billy do but begin right
there on the grass the kind of a tussle we
always have in the big rocking-chair on
the porch! Over and over we rolled, Billy
chuckling and squealing while I laughed
myself all out of breath. I'm glad I always would wear delicious petticoats, for
there, looking right over my front fence,
I discovered Judge Benton Wade. I wish
I could write down how I felt, for I never
had that sensation before and I don't believe I'll ever have it again.

I have always thought that Judge
Wade was really the most wonderful man
in Hillsboro, not because he is a judge so

young in life that there is only a white
sprinkle in his lovely black hair that grows
back off his head like Napoleon's and
Charles Wesley's, but because of his smile,
which you wait for so long that you glow
all over when you get it. I have seen him
do it once or twice at his mother when he
seats her in their pew at church and once
at little Mamie Johnson when she gave
him a flower through their fence as he
passed by one day last week, but I never
thought I should have one all to myself.
But there it was, a most beautiful one,
long and slow and distinctly mine—at
least I didn't think much of it was for
Billie. I sat up and blushed as red all
over as I do when I first hit that tub of
cold water.

"I hope you'll forgive an intruder, Mrs.
Carter, but how could a mortal resist a
peep into the garden of the gods if he

28

I sat up and blushed red all over

spied the queen and her faun at play?" he said in a voice as wonderful as the smile. By that time I had reefed in my ruffles around my feet and pushed in all my hairpins. Billy stood spread-legged as near in front of me as he could get and said in the rudest possible tone of voice:

"Get away from my Molly, man!"

I never was so mortified in all my life and I scrambled to my feet and came over to the fence to get between him and Billy.

"It's a lovely day, isn't it, Judge Wade?" I asked with the greatest interest, which I didn't really feel, in the weather; but what could I think of to say? A woman is apt to keep the image of a good many of the grand men she sees passing around her in queer niches in her brain, and when one steps out and speaks to her for the first time it is confusing. Of course I have known the judge and his

mother all my life, for she is one of Aunt
Adeline's best friends, but I had a feeling
from the look in his eyes that that very
minute was the first time he had ever seen
me. It was lovely and I blushed some
more as I put my hand up to my cheek so
I wouldn't have to look right at him.

"About the loveliest day that ever happened in Hillsboro," he said, and there
was still more of the delicious smile,
"though I hadn't noticed it so especially
until—"

But I never knew what he had intended
to say, for Billy suddenly swelled up like
a little turkey-cock and cut out with his
switch at the judge.

"Git, man, git, and let my Molly alone!"
he said, in a perfect thundertone of voice;
but I almost laughed, for it had such a
sound in it like Doctor John's at his most
positive times with Billy and me.

A LOVE-LETTER, LOADED

"No, no, Billy, the judge is just looking over the fence at our flowers! Don't
you want to give him a rose?" I hurried
to say as the smile died out of Judge
Wade's face and he looked at Billy in-
tently.

"How like John Moore the youngster
is," he said, and his voice was so cold to
Billy that it hurt me, and I was afraid
Billy would notice it. Coldness in people's
voices always makes me feel just like ice-
cream tastes. But Billy's answer was still
more rude.

"You better go, man, before I bring my
father to sic our dog on you," he ex-
ploded, and before I could stop him his
thin little legs went trundling down the
garden path toward home.

Then the judge and I both laughed.
We couldn't help it. When two people
laugh straight into each other's eyes

something feels dangerous and you get closer together. The judge leaned farther over the fence and I went a little nearer before I knew it.

"You don't need to keep a personal dog, do you, Mrs. Carter?" he asked, with a twinkle that might have been a spark in his eyes, and just at that moment another awful thing happened. Aunt Adeline came out on the front porch and said in the most frozen tone of voice:

"Mary, I wish to speak to you in the house," and then walked back through the front door without even looking in Judge Wade's direction, though he had waved his hat with one of his mother's own smiles when he had seen her before I did. One of my most impossible habits is, when there is nothing else to do I laugh. I did it then and it saved the day, for we both laughed into each others eyes a second time, and before we realized it we were within whispering distance.

"No, I don't—don't—need any dog," I said softly, hardly glancing out from under my lashes because I was afraid to risk looking straight at him again so soon. I could fairly feel Aunt Adeline's eyes boring into my back.

"It would take the hydra-headed monster of—may I bring my mother to call on you and the—Mrs. Henderson?" he asked and poured the wonder smile all over me. Again I almost caught my breath.

"I do wish you would, Aunt Adeline is so fond of Mrs. Wade!" I said in a positive flutter that I hope he didn't see, but I am afraid he did, for he hesitated as if he wanted to say something to calm me, then bowed mercifully and went on down the street. He didn't put on the hat he had held in his hand all the while he stood by the fence until he had looked back and bowed again. Then I felt still more fluttered as I went into the house, but I received the third cold plunge of the day when I reached the front hall.

"Mary," said Aunt Adeline in a voice that sounded as if it had been buried and never resurrected, "if you are going to continue in such an unseemly course of conduct I hope you will remove your mourning, which is an empty mockery and an insult to my own widowhood."

"Yes, Aunt Adeline, I'll go take it off this very minute," I heard myself answer her airily to my own astonishment. I might have known that if I ever got one of those smiles it would go to my head! Without another word I sailed into my room and closed the door softly.

I wonder if God could have realized

what a tender thing He was leaving exposed to life in the garden of the world after He had finished making a woman? Traditionally, we are created out of rose-leaves and star-dust and the harmony of the winds, but we need a steel-chain netting to fend us. Slowly I unbuttoned that black dress that symbolized the ending of six years of the blackness of a married life, from which I had been powerless to fend myself, and the rosy dimpling thing in snowy lingerie with tags of blue ribbon that stood in front of my mirror was as new-born as any other hour-old similar bundle of linen and lace in Hillsboro, Tennessee. Fortunately, an old, year-before-last, white lawn dress could be pulled from the top shelf of the closet in a hurry, and the Molly that came out of that room was ready for life—and a lot of it quick and fast.

35

And again, fortunately, Aunt Adeline had retired with a violent headache and black Judy was carrying her in a hot water-bottle with a broad grin on her face. Judy sees the world from the kitchen window and understands everything. She had laid a large thick letter on the hall table where I couldn't fail to see it.

I took possession of it and carried it to a bench in the garden that backs up against the purple sprayed lilacs and is flanked by two rows of tall purple and white iris that stand in line ready for a Virginia reel with a delicate row of the poet's narcissus across the broad path. I love my flowers. I love them swaying on their stems in the wind, and I like to snatch them and crush the life out of them against my breast and face. I have been to bed every night this spring with a

36

bunch of cool violets against my cheek
and I feel that I am going to flirt with my
tall row of hollyhocks as soon as they are
old enough to hold up their heads and
take notice. They always remind me of
very stately gentlemen and I have wondered if the fluffy little butter and eggs
weren't shaking their ruffles at them.

A real love-letter ought to be like a
cream puff with a drop of dynamite in it.
Alfred's was that kind. I felt warm and
happy down to my toes as I read it and
I turned around so old Lilac Bush couldn't
peep over my shoulder at what he said.

He wrote from Rome this time, where
he had been sent on some sort of dip-
lomatic mission to the Vatican, and his
letter about the Ancient City on her seven
hills was a prose-poem in itself. I was so
interested that I read on and on and forgot it was almost toast-apple time.

Of course, anybody that is anybody would be interested in Father Tiber and the old Colosseum, but what made me forget the one slice of dry toast and the apple was the way he seemed to be connecting me up with all those wonderful old antiquities that had never even seen me. Because of me he had felt and written that poem descriptive of old Tiber, and the moonlight had lit up the Colosseum just because I was over here lighting up Hillsboro, Tennessee, with Mr. Carter dead. Of course that is not the way he put it all, but there is no place to really copy what he did say down into this imp book and, anyway, that is the sentiment he expressed, boiled down and sugared off.

That's just what I mean—love boiled down and sugared off is mighty apt to get an explosive flavor, and one had better be careful with that kind if one is timid;

which I'm not. As I said, also, I am
ready for a little taste of life, so I read on
without fear. And, to be fair, Alfred
had well boiled his own last paragraph.
It snapped; and I jumped and gasped
both. I almost thought I didn't quite like
it and was going to read it over again to
see, when there came a procession from
over to Doctor John's and I laid the bomb-
shell down on the bench.

First came the red setter that is always
first with Doctor John, and then he came
himself, leading Billy by the hand. It was
Billy, but the most subdued Billy I ever
saw, and I held out my arms and started
for him.

"Wait a minute, please, Molly," said
the doctor in the voice he always uses
when he's punishing Billy and me. "Bill
came to apologize to you for being rude to
your—your guest. He told me all about

it and I think he's sorry. Tell Mrs. Carter you are sorry, son." When that man speaks to me as if I were just any old body else, I hate him so it is a wonder I don't show it more than I do. But there was nothing to say and I looked at Billy and Billy looked at me.

Then suddenly he stretched out his little arms to me and the dimples winked at me from all over his darling face.

"Molly, Molly," he said with a perfect rapture of chuckles in his voice, "now you look just as pretty as you do when you go to bed; all whity all over. You can kiss my kiss-spot a hundred times while I bear-hug you for that nice not-black dress," and before any stern person could have stopped us I was on my knees on the grass kissing my fill from the "kiss-spot" on the back of his neck, while he

40

hugged all the starch out of the summer-before-last.

And Doctor John sat down on the bench quick and laughed out loud one of the very few times I ever heard him do it. He was looking down at us, but I didn't laugh up into *his* eyes. I was afraid. I felt it was safer to go on kissing the kiss-spot for the present, anyway.

"Bill," he said, with his voice dancing, "that's the most effective apology I ever heard. You were sorry to some point."

Then suddenly Billy stiffened right in my arms and looked me straight in the face and said in the doctor's own brisk tones, even with his cupid mouth set in the same straight line:

"I say I'm sorry, Molly, but damn that man and I'll git him yet!"

What could we say? What could we

do? We didn't try. I busied myself in tying the string on Billy's blouse that had come untied in the bear-hug and the doctor suddenly discovered the letter on the bench. I saw him see it without looking in his direction at all.

"And how many pounds are we nearer the string-bean state of existence, Mrs. Molly?" he asked me before I had finished tying the blouse, in the nicest voice in the world, fairly crackling with friendship and good humor and hateful things like that. Why I should have wanted him to huff over that letter is more than I can say. But I did; and he didn't.

"Over twenty, and most of the time I am so hungry I could eat Aunt Adeline. I dream about Billy, fried with cream gravy," I answered, as I kissed again the back of the head that was beginning to nod down against my breast. Long shadows lay across the garden and the white-headed old snow-ball was signaling out of the dusk to a Dorothy Perkins down the walk in a scandalous way. At best, spring is just the world's match-making old chaperon and ought to be watched. I still sat on the grass and I began to cuddle Billy's bare knees in the skirt of my dress so the chigres couldn't get at them.

"But, Mrs. Molly, isn't it worth it all?" asked the doctor as he bent over toward us and looked down with something wonderful and kind in his eyes that seemed to rest on us like a benediction. "You have been just as plucky as a girl can be and in only a little over two months you have grown as lightfooted and hearty as a boy. *I* think nothing could be lovelier than you are right now, but you can get off those other few pounds if you want to. You know, don't you, that I have known how hard some of it was and I haven't been able to eat as much as I usually do thinking how hungry you are? But isn't it all worth it? I think it is. Alfred Bennett is a very great man and it is right that he should have a very lovely wife to go out into the world with him. And as lovely as you are I think it is wonderful of you to make all this sacrifice to be still lovelier for him. I am glad I can help you and it has taught me something to see how—how faithful a woman can be across years —and then in this smaller thing! Now give me Bill and you get your apple and toast. Don't forget to take your letter in out of the dew." I sat perfectly still and held Billy tighter in my arms as I looked up at his father, and then after I had thought as long as I could stand it, I spoke right out at him as mad as hops and I don't to this minute know why.

A LOVE-LETTER, LOADED

"Nobody in the world ever doubted that a woman could be faithful if she had anything to be faithful to," I said as I let him take Billy out of my arms at last. "Faithfulness is what a woman flowers, only it takes a *man* to pick his posy." With which I marched into the house and left him standing with Billy in his arms, I hope dumfounded. I didn't look back to see. I always leave that man's presence so mad I can never look back at him. And wouldn't it make any woman rage to have a man pick out another man for her to be faithful to when she hadn't made any decision about it her own self?

I wonder just how old Judge Wade is? I believe I will make up with Aunt Adeline enough before I go to bed to find out why he has never married.

LEAF THIRD

MEN are very strange people. They are like those horrible sums in algebra that you think about and worry about and cry about and try to get help from other women about, and then, all of a sudden, X works itself out into perfectly good sense. Not that I thought much about Mr. Carter, poor man! When he wasn't right around I felt it best to forget him as much as I could, but it seems hard for other women to let you forget either your husband or theirs.

I know now that I really never got any older than the poor, foolish, eighteen-years' child that Aunt Adeline married off "safe", all the time I was the "refuge" sort of wife. I would sit and listen while the other wives talked over the men in utter bewilderment and most times terror, then I would force myself to a little more forgetting and poor Mr. Carter must have suffered the consequences. But all that was a mild sort of exasperation to what a widow has to go through with in the matter of—of, well I think hazing is about the best name to give it.

"Molly Carter," said Mrs. Johnson just day before yesterday, after the white-dress, Judge-Wade episode that Aunt Adeline had gone to all the friends up and down the street to be consoled about, "if you haven't got sense enough to appreciate your present blissful condition somebody ought to operate on your mind."

I was tempted to say, "Why not my heart?" I was glad she didn't know how

47

good that heart did feel under my tucker when the boy brought that basket of fish from Judge Wade's fishing trip Saturday. I have firmly determined not to blush any more at the thought of that gorgeous man —at least outwardly.

"Don't you think it is very—very lonely to be a widow, Mrs. Johnson?" I asked timidly to see what she would say about Mr. Johnson, who is really lovely, I think. He gives me the gentlest understanding smile when he meets me on the street of late weeks.

"Lonely, *lonely,* Molly? You talk about the married state exactly like an old maid. Don't do it—it's foolish, and you will get the lone notion really fastened in your mind and let some fool man find out that is how you feel. Then it will be all over with you. I have only one regret, and it is that if I ever should be a widow

Mr. Johnson wouldn't be here to see how quickly I turned into an old maid, by the grace of God." Mrs. Johnson sews by assassinating the cloth with the needle, and as she talked she was mending the sleeve of one of Mr. Johnson's shirts.

"I think an old maid is just a woman who has never been in love with a man who loves her. Lots of them have been married for years," I said, just as innocently as the soft face of a pan of cream, and went on darning one of Billy's socks.

"Well, be that as it may, they are the blessed members of the women tribe," she answered, looking at me sharply. "Now I have often told Mr. Johnson—" but here we were interrupted in what might have been the rehearsal of a glorious scrap by the appearance of Aunt Bettie Pollard, and with her came a long, tall, lovely vision of a woman in the most wonderful

close clingy dress and hat that you wanted
to eat on sight. I hated her instantly with
the most intense adoration that made me
want to lie down at her feet, and also
made me feel like I had gained all the
more than twenty pounds that I have
slaved off me and doubled them on again.
I would have liked to lead her that minute
into Doctor John's office and just to have
looked at him and said one word—
"string-bean!" Aunt Betty introduced
her as Miss Chester from Washington.

"Oh, my dear Mrs. Carter, how glad I
am to meet you!" she said as she towered
over me in a willowy way, and her voice
was lovely and cool almost to slimness.
"I am the bearer of so many gracious
messages that I am anxious to deliver
them safely to you. Not six weeks ago
I left Alfred Bennett in Paris and really
—really his greetings to you almost

amounted to steamer luggage. He came down to Cherbourg to see me off, and almost the last thing he said to me was, 'Now, don't fail to see Mrs. Carter as soon as you get to Hillsboro; and the more you see of her the more you'll enjoy your visit to Mrs. Pollard.' Isn't he the most delightful of men?" She asked me the question, but she had the most wonderful way of seeming to be talking to everybody at one time, so Mrs. Johnson got in the first answer.

"Delightful, nothing! But Al Bennett is a man of sense not to marry any of the string of women I suppose he's got following him!" she said. Miss Chester looked at her in a mild kind of wonder, but she went on murdering Mr. Johnson's shirt-sleeve with the needle without noticing the glance at all.

"Well, well, honey, I don't know about

that," said Aunt Bettie as she fanned and
rocked her great, big, darling, fat self in
the strong rocker I always kept in the
breezy angle of the porch for her. "Al
is not old enough to have proved himself
entirely, and from what I hear—" she
paused with the big hearty smile that she
always wears when she begins to tease or
match-make, and she does them both most
of her time.

But at whom do you suppose she
looked? Not me! Miss Chester! That
was cold tub number two for that day,
and I didn't react as quickly as I might,
but when I did I was in the proper glow
all over. When I revived and saw the
lovely pale blush on her face I felt like a
cabbage-rose beside a tea-bud. I was
glad Aunt Adeline came out on the porch
just then so I could go in and tell Judy
to bring out the iced tea and cakes. When

MONUMENT OR TROUSSEAU?

I came from the kitchen I stepped into my room and took out one of Alfred's letters from the desk drawer and opened it at random, as you do the Bible when you want to decide things, and put my finger down on a line with my eyes shut. This was what it was:

"—and all these years I have walked the world, blindfolded to its loveliness with the blackness that came to me when I found that you—"

I didn't read any more, but shoved it back in a hurry and went on out on the porch, comforted in a way, but feeling some more in sympathy with Mrs Johnson than I had before Aunt Bettie and her guest from Washington had interrupted our algebraic demonstration on the man subject. You can't always be sure of the right answer to X in any proposition of life; that is, a woman can't!

And, furthermore, I didn't like that next hour much, just as a sample of life, for instance. Aunt Bettie had got her joining-together humor well started, and right there before my face she made a present of every nice man in Hillsboro to that lovely, distinguished, strange girl who could have slipped through a bucket hoop if she had tried hard. I had to sit there, listen to the presentations, watch her drink two tall delicious glasses of tea full of sugar and consume without fear three of Judy's puffy cakes, while I crumbled mine in secret over the banisters and set half the glass of tea out of sight behind the wistaria vine.

It was bad enough to hear Aunt Bettie just offer her Tom, who, if he is her own son, is my favorite cousin, but I believe the worst minute I almost ever faced was when she began on the judge, for I could

see from Aunt Adeline's shoulder beyond
Miss Chester how she was enjoying that,
and she added another distinguished an-
cestor to his pedigree every time Aunt
Bettie paused for breath. I couldn't say
a word about the fish and Aunt Adeline
wouldn't! I almost loved Mrs. Johnson
when she bit off a thread viciously and
said, "Humph," as she rose to start the
tea-party home.

That night I did so many exercises
that at last I sank exhausted in a chair
in front of my mirror and put my head
down on my arms and cried the real tears
you cry when nobody is looking. I felt
terribly old and ugly and dowdy and—
widowed. It couldn't have been jealousy,
for I just love that girl. I want most
awfully to hug her very slimness and it
was more what she might think of poor
dumpy me than what any man in Hills-

boro, Tennessee, or Paris, France, could possibly feel on the subject that hurt so hard. But then, looking back on it, I am afraid that jealousy sheds feathers every night so you won't know him in the morning, for something made me sit up suddenly with a spark in my eyes and reach out to the desk for my pencil and check-book. It took me more than an hour to figure it all up, but I went to bed a happier, though in prospects a poorer woman.

It is strange how spending a man's money makes you feel more congenial with him and as I sat in the cars on my way to the city early the next morning I felt nearer to Mr. Carter than I almost ever did, alive or dead. After this I shall always appreciate and admire him for the way he made money, since, for the first time in my life, I

I was spellbound with delight

fully realized what it could buy. And I bought things!

First I went to see Madam Courtier for corsets. I had heard about her and I knew it meant a fortune. But that didn't matter! She came in and looked at me for about five minutes without saying a word and then she ran her hands down and down over me until I could feel the flesh just crawling off of me. It was delicious!

Then she and two girls in puffs and rats came in and did things to a corset they laced on me that I can't even write down, for I didn't understand the process, but when I looked in that long glass I almost dropped on the floor. I wasn't tight and I wasn't stiff and I looked—I'm too modest to write how lovely I really looked to myself. I was spellbound with delight.

Next I signed the check for three of those wonders with my head so in the clouds I didn't know what I was doing, but I came to with a jolt when the prettiest girl began to get me into that black taffeta bag I had worn down to the city. I must have shrunk the whole remaining pounds I had felt obliged to lose for Alfred and Ruth Chester from the horror I felt when I looked at myself. The girl was really sympathetic and said with a smile that was true kindness: "Shall I call a taxi for madam and have it take her to Klein's? They have wonderful gowns by Rene all ready to be fitted at short notice. Really, madam's figure is such that it commands a perfect costume now." Men do business well, but when women enter the field they are geniuses at money extracting. I felt myself already clothed perfectly when that girl said my figure "commanded" a proper dress. Of course, Klein pays Madam Courtier a commission for the customers she passes right on to him. The one for me must have looked to her like a real estate transaction.

I spent three days at the great Klein store, only going to the hotel to sleep and most of the time I forgot to eat. Madam Rene must have been Madam Courtier's twin sister in youth, and Madam Telliers in the hat department was the triplet to them both. When women have genius it breaks out all over them like measles and they never recover from it; those women had the confluent kind. But I know that old Rene really liked me, for when I blushed and asked her if they had a good beauty doctor in the store she held up her hands and shuddered.

"Never, Madam, never *pour vous.*

Ravissant, charmant—it is to fool. Nevair! *Jamais, jamais de la vie!*" I had to calm her down and she kissed my hand when we parted.

I thought Klein was going to do the same thing or worse when I signed the check which would be good for a house and lot and motor-car for him, but he didn't. Only he got even with me by saying: "And I am delighted that the trousseau is perfectly satisfactory to you, Mrs. Carter."

That was an awful shock and I hope I didn't show it as I murmured: "Perfectly, thank you."

The word "trousseau" can be spoken in a woman's presence for many years with no effect, but it is an awful shock when she first *really* hears it. I felt funny all afternoon as I packed those trunks for the five o'clock train.

MONUMENT OR TROUSSEAU?

Yes, the word "trousseau" ought to have a definite surname after it always and that's why my loyalty dragged poor Mr. Carter out into the light of my conscience. The thinking of him had a strange effect on me. I had laid out the dream in dark gray-blue rajah, tailored almost beyond endurance; to wear home on the train and had thrown the old black taffeta bag across the chair to give to the hotel maid, but the decision of the session between conscience and loyalty made me pack the precious blue wonder and put on once more the black rags of remembrance in a kind of panic of respect.

I would lots rather have bought poor Mr. Carter the monument I have been planning for months to keep up conversation with Aunt Adeline, than wear that dress again. I felt conscience reprove me once more with loyalty looking on in dis-

approval as I buttoned the old thing up
for the last time, because I really ought
to have stayed over a day to buy that
monument, but—to tell the truth I wanted
to see Billy so desperately that his "sleep-
place" above my heart hurt as if it might
have prickly heat break out at any minute.

So I hurried and stuffed the gray-blue
darling in the top tray, lapped old black
taffeta around my waist and belted it in
with a black belt off a new green linen I
had made for morning walks, down to
the drug store on the public square, I suppose. That is about the only morning dissipation in Hillsboro that I can think of,
and it all depends on whom you meet,
how much of a dissipation it is.

The next thing that happens after you
have done a noble deed is, you either re-
gard it as a reward of virtue or as a pun-

ishment for having been foolish. I felt both ways when Judge Wade came down the car aisle, looking so much grander than any other man in sight that I don't see how they stand him ever. At that minute the noble black-taffeta deed felt foolish, but at the next minute I thanked my lucky stars for it.

It is nice to watch for a person to catch sight of you if you feel sure how they are going to take it and somehow in this case I felt sure. I was not disappointed, for his smile broke his face up into a joy-laugh. Off came his hat instantly so I could catch a glimpse of the fascinating frost over his temples, and with a positive sigh of rapture he subsided into the seat beside me. I turned with an echo smile all over me when suddenly his face became grave and considerate, and he looked at me as all the men in Hillsboro have been doing ever since poor Mr. Carter's funeral.

"Mrs. Carter," he said very kindly, in a voice that pitched me out of the car window and left me a mile behind on the track, all by myself, "I wish I had known of your sad errand to town so I could have offered you some assistance in your selection. You know we have just had our lot in the cemetery finally arranged and I found the dealers in memorial stones very confusing in their ideas and designs. Mrs. Henderson just told my mother of your absence from home last night, and I could only come down to the city for the day on important business or I would have arranged to see you. I hope you found something that satisfied you."

What's a woman going to say when she has a tombstone thrown in her face like that? I didn't say anything, but what I thought about Aunt Adeline filled in a dreadful pause.

Perfectly dumb and quiet I sat for an awful space of time and wondered just what I was going to do. Could a woman lie a monument into her suit case? It was beyond me at that speaking and the Molly that is ready for life quick, didn't want to. I shut my eyes, counted three to myself as I do when I go over into the cold tub, and told him all about it. We both got a satisfactory reaction and I never enjoyed myself so much as that before.

I understand now why Judge Wade has had so many women martyr themselves over him and live unhappily ever afterward, as everybody says Henrietta Mason is doing. He's a very inspiring man and he fairly bristles with fascinations. Some men are what you call taking and they take you if they want you, while others are drawing and after you are drawn to them they will consider the question of taking you. The judge is like that.

In the meantime it tingles me up to a very great degree to have a man use his eyes on me as it is the privilege of only womankind to do, and I feel that it will be good for his judgeship for me to let him "draw" me at least a little way. I may get hurt, but I shall at least have an interesting time of it. I started right then and got results, for he stopped under the old lilac bush that leans over my side gate and kissed my hand. Old Lilac shook a laugh of perfume all over us and I believe signaled the event at the top of his bough to the white clump on the other side of the garden. I'm glad Aunt Adeline isn't in the flower fraternity or sorority. Suppose she had seen or heard!

MONUMENT OR TROUSSEAU?

And it didn't take many minutes for me to slip into old summer-before-last— also for the last time inside of those buttons—and run through the garden, my heart singing, "Billy, Billy," in a perfect rapture of tune. I ran past the office door and found him in his cot almost asleep and we had a bear reunion in the rocker by the window that made us both breathless.

"What did you bring me, Molly?" he finally kissed under my right ear.

"A real base-ball and bat, lover, and an engine with five cars, a rake and a spade and a hoe, two blow-guns that pop a new way and something that squirts water and some other things. Will that be enough?" I hugged him up anxiously, for sometimes he is hard to please and I might not have got the very thing he wanted.

"Thank you, Molly, all them things is

what I want, but you oughter brung more'n that for three days not being here with me." Did any woman ever have a more lovely lover than that? I don't know how long I should have rocked him in the twilight if Doctor John's voice hadn't come across the hall in command.

"Put him down now, Mrs. Molly, and come and say other how-do-you-does," he called softly.

It was a funny glad-to-see-him I felt as I came into the office where he was standing over by the window looking out at my garden in its twilight glow. I think it is wrong for a woman to let her imagination kiss a man on the back of his neck even if she has known for some time that there is a little drake-tail lock of hair there just like his own son's. I gave him my hand and a good deal more of a smile and a blush than I intended.

68

MONUMENT OR TROUSSEAU?

He very far from kissed the hand; he held it just long enough to turn me around into the light and give me one long looking-over from head to feet.

"Just where does that corset press you worst?" he asked in the tone of voice he uses to say "poke out your tongue." So much of my Tennessee shooting-blood rose to my face that it is a wonder it didn't drip; but I was cold enough to have hit at forty paces if I had had a shooting-iron in my hand. As it was the coldness was the only missile that I had, but I used it to some effect.

"I am making a call on a friend, Doctor Moore, and not a consultation visit to my physician," I said, looking into his face as though I had never seen him before.

"I beg your pardon, Molly," he exclaimed and his face was redder than

mine and then it went white with morti-
fication. I couldn't stand that.

"Don't do that way!" I exclaimed, and
before I knew it I had taken hold of his
hand and had it in both of mine. "I know
I look as if I was shrunk or laced, but
I'm not! I was going to tell you all about
it and show it to you. I'm really inches
bigger in the right place and just—just
'controlled', the woman called it, in the
wrong place. Please feel me and see,"
and I offered myself to him for examina-
tion in the most regardless way. He's not
at all like other people.

The blood came back into his face and
he laughed as he gave me a little shake
that pushed me away from him. "Don't
you ever scare me like that again, child,
or it might be serious," he said in the
Billy-and-me tone of voice that I like
some, only—

"I never will," I said in a hurry; "I want you to ask me anything in the world you want to and I'll always do it."

"Well, let me take you home through the garden then—and, yes, I believe I'll stay to break a muffin with Mrs. Henderson. Don't you want to tell me what a little girl like you did in a big city and—and read me part of that London letter I saw the postman give Judy this afternoon?"

Again I ask myself the question why his friendliness to Alfred Bennett's letters always makes me so instantly cross.

LEAF FOURTH

SCATTERED JAM

SLEEP is one of the most delightful and undervalued amusements known to the human race. I have never had enough yet and every second of time that I'm not busy with something interesting I curl up on the bed and go dream hunting—only I sleep too hard to do much catching. But this torture book found that out on me and stopped it the very first thing on page three. The command is to sleep as little as possible to keep the nerves in a good condition,—"eight hours at the most and seven would be better." What earthly good would a seven-hour nap do me? I want ten hours to sleep and twelve if I get a good tired start. To see me stagger out of my perfectly nice bed at six o'clock every morning now would wring the sternest heart with compassion and admiration at my faithfulness—to whom?

Yes, it was the day after poor Mr. Carter's funeral that Aunt Adeline moved up here into my house and settled herself in the big south room across the hall from mine. Her furniture weighs a ton each piece, and Aunt Adeline is not light herself in disposition. The next morning when I went in to breakfast she sat in the "vacant chair" in a way that made me see that she was obviously trying to fill the vacancy. I am sorry she worried herself about that. Anyway, it made me take a resolve. After breakfast I went into the kitchen to speak to Judy.

"Judy," I said, looking past her head,

73

"my health is not very good and you can bring my breakfast to me in bed after this." Poor Mr. Carter always wanted breakfast on the stroke of seven, and me at the same time, though he rarely got me. Judy has two dead husbands and she likes a ginger-colored barber down-town. Also her mother is our washerwoman and influenced by Aunt Adeline. Judy understands everything I say to her. After I had closed the door I heard a laugh that sounded like a war-whoop, and I smiled to myself. But that was before my martyrdom to this book had begun. I get up now!

But the day after I came from the city I lay in bed just as long as I wanted to and ignored the thought of the exercises and deep breathing and the icy unsympathetic tub. I couldn't even take very much interest in the lonely egg on the lonely slice of dry toast. I was thinking about things.

Hillsboro is a very peculiar little speck on the universe; even more peculiar than being like a hen. It is one of the oldest towns in Tennessee and the moss on it is so thick that it can't be scratched off except in spots. But it has a lot of race-horse and distillery money in it and when it gets poked up by anything unusual it takes a gulp of its own alcoholic atmosphere and runs away on its own track at a two-five gait, shedding moss as it goes. It hasn't had a real joy-race for a long time and I felt that it needed it. I rolled over and laughed into my pillow.

The subject of the conduct of widows is a serious one. Of all the things old Tradition is most set about it is that, and what was decided to be the proper thing a million years ago this town still dictates shall be done, and spends a good deal of its time seeing its directions carried out. For a year after the funeral they forget about the poor bereaved and when they do remember her they speak to and of her in the same tones of voice they used at the obsequies. Then sooner or later some neighbor is sure to see some man walk home from church with her or hear some old bachelor's voice on her front porch. Mr. Cain took Mrs. Caruther's little Jessie up in his buggy and helped her out at her mother's gate just before last Christmas, and if the poor widow hadn't acted quick the town would have noticed them to death before he proposed to her. They were married the day after New Year's and she lost lots of good friends because she didn't give them more time to talk about it.

I don't intend to run any risk of losing

my friends that way and I want them to
have all the good time they can get out of
it. I'm going to serve out mint-juleps of
excitement until the dear old place is running as it did when it was a two-year-old.
Why get mad when people are interested
in you? It's a compliment after all and
just gives them more to think about. I
remembered the two trunks across the hall
and hugged my knees up under by chin
with pleasure at the thought of the town-
talk they contained.

Then just as I had got the first plan
well-going and was deciding whether to
wear the mauve meteor or the white chif-
fon with the rosebud embroidery as a first
julep for my friends, a sweetness came in
through my window that took my breath
away and I lay still with my hand over
my heart and listened. It was Billy singing right under my window, and I've

never heard him do it before in all his five years. It was the dearest old-fashioned tune ever written and Billy sang the words as distinctly as if he had been a boy chorister doing a difficult recitative. My heart beat so it shook the lace on my breast like a breeze from heaven as he took the high note and then let it go on the last few words.

"If you love me, Molly, darling,
Let your answer be a kiss!"

A confused recollection of having heard the words and tune sung by my mother when I was at the rocking age myself brought the tears to my eyes as I flew to the window and parted the curtains. If you heard a little boy-angel singing at your casement wouldn't you expect a cherubim face upturned with heaven-lights all over it? Billy's face was up-

I lifted him into my arms

turned as he heard me draw the shade, but it was streaked like a wild Indian's with decorations of brown mud and he held a long slimy fish-worm on the end of a stick while he wiped his other grimy hand down the front of his linen blouse.

"Say, Molly, look at the snake I brunged you!" he exclaimed as he came close under the sill, which is not high from the ground. "If you put your face down to the mud and sing something to 'em they'll come outen they holes. A doodle-bug comed, too, but I couldn't ketch 'em both. Lift me up and I can put him in the water-glass on your table." He held up one muddy paddie to me and promptly I lifted him up into my arms. From the embrace in which he and the worm and I indulged my lace and dimity came out much the worse.

"That was a lovely song you sang about

'Molly, darling', Billy," I said. "Where did you hear it?"

"That's a good bug-song, Molly, and I bet I can git a lizard with it, too, if I sing it right low." He began to squirm out of my arms toward the table and the glass.

"Who taught it to you, sugar-sweet?" I persisted as I poured water in on the squirming worm under his direction.

"Nobody taught it to me. Doc sings it to me when Tilly, nurse, nor you ain't there to put me to bed. He don't know no good songs like *Roll, Jordan, Roll,* or *Hot Times* or *Twinkle*. I go to sleep quick 'cause he makes me feel tired with his slow tune what's only good for bugs. Git a hair-pin for me to poke him with, Molly, quick!"

I found the hair-pin and I don't know why my hand trembled as I handed it to

Billy. As soon as he got it he climbed out the window, glass, bug and all, and I saw him and the red setter go down the garden walk together in pursuit of the desired lizard, I suppose. I closed the blinds and drew the curtains again and flung myself on my pillow. Something warm and sweet seemed to be sweeping over me in great waves and I felt young and close up to some sort of big world-good. It was delicious and I don't know how long I would have stayed there just feeling it if Judy hadn't brought in my letter.

He had written from London, and it was many pages of wonderful things all flavored with me. He told me about Miss Chester and what good friends they were, and how much he hoped she would be in Hillsboro when he got here. He said that a great many of her dainty ways re-

minded him of his "own slip of a girl",
especially the turn of her head like a
"flower on its stem." At that I got right
out of bed like a jack jumping out of a
box and looked at myself in the mirror.

There is one exercise here on page
twenty that I hate worst of all. You
screw up your face tight until you look
like a Christmas mask to get your neck
muscles taut and then wobble your head
around like a new-born baby until it
swims. I did that one twenty extra times
and all the others in proportion to make
up for those two hours in bed. Here-
after I'll get up at the time directed on
page three, or maybe earlier. It frightens
me to think that I've got only a few weeks
more to turn from a cabbage-rose into a
lily. I won't let myself even think "luscious peach" and "string-bean." If I do,
I get warm and happy all over and let up

on myself. I try when I get hungry to
think of myself in that blue muslin dress.

I haven't been really willing before to
write down in this torture volume that I
took that garment to the city with me and
what Madam Rene did to it—made it
over into the loveliest thing I ever saw,
only I wouldn't let her alter the size one
single inch. I'm honorable as all women
are at peculiar times. I think she understood, but she seemed not to, and worked
a miracle on it with ribbon and lace. I've
put it away on the top shelf of a closet,
for it is torment to look at it.

You can just take any old recipe for
a party and mix up a début for a girl, but
it takes more time to concoct one for a
widow, especially if it is for yourself. I
spent all the rest of the day doing almost
nothing and thinking until I felt light-
headed. Finally I had just about given

up any idea of a blaze and had decided to leak out in general society as quietly as my clothes would let me, when a real conflagration was lighted inside me.

If Tom Pollard wasn't my own first cousin I would have loved him desperately, even if I am a week older than he. He was about the only oasis in my marriage mirage, though I don't think anybody would think of calling him at all green. He never stopped coming to see me occasionally, and Mr. Carter liked him. He was the first man to notice the white ruche I sewed in the neck of my old black taffeta four or five months ago and he let me see that he noticed it out of the corner of his eyes even right there in church, under Aunt Adeline's very elbow. He makes love unconsciously and he flirts with his own mother. As soon as I've made this widowhood hurdle—well, I'm

going to spend a lot of time buying tobacco with him in his Hup runabout, which
sounds as if it was named for himself.

And when that conflagration was
lighted in me about my début, Tom did
it. I was sitting peaceably on my own
front steps, dressed in the summer-before-last that Judy washes and irons
every day while I'm deciding how to hand
out the first sip of my trousseau to the
neighbors, when Tom, in a dangerous
blue-striped shirt, with a tie that melted
into it in tone, blew over my hedge and
landed at my side. He kissed the lace
ruffle on my sleeve while I reproved him
severely and settled down to enjoy him.
But I didn't have such an awfully good
time as I generally do with him. He was
too full of another woman, and even a
first cousin can be an exasperation in that
condition.

"Now, Mrs. Molly, truly did you ever see such a peach as she is?" he demanded after I had expressed more than a dozen delighted opinions of Miss Chester. His use of the word "peach" riled me and before I stopped to think, I said: "She reminds me more of a string-bean."

"Now, Molly, don't be mean just because old Wade has got her out driving behind the grays after kissing your hand under the lilacs yesterday, which, praise be, nobody saw but little me! I'm not sore, why should you be? Aren't you happy with me?"

I withered him with a look, or rather *tried* to wither him, for Tom is no Mimosa bud.

"The way that girl has started in to wake up this little old town reminds me of the feeling you get under your belt seven minutes after you've sipped an ab-

86

sinthe frappé for the first time—you are liable for a good jag and don't know it," he continued enthusiastically. "Let's don't let the folks know that they are off until I get everybody in a full swing of buzz over my queen." I had never seen Tom so enthusiastic over a girl before and I didn't like it. But I decided not to let him know that, but to get to work putting out the Chester blaze in him and starting one on my own account.

"That's just what I'm thinking about, Tom," I said with a smile that was as sweet as I could make it, "and as she came with messages to me from one of my best old friends I think I ought to do something to make her have a good time. I was just planning a gorgeous dinner-party I want to have for her when you came so suddenly. Do you think we could arrange it for Tuesday evening?"

"Lord love us, Molly, don't knock the town down like that! Let 'em have more than a week to get used to this white rag of a dress you've been waving in their faces for the last few days. Go slow!"

"I've been going so slow for so many years that I've turned around and I'm going fast backward," I said with a blush that I couldn't help.

"Help! Let my kinship protect me!" exclaimed Tom in alarm, and he pretended to move an inch away from me.

"Yes," I said slowly and as I looked out of the corner of my eyes from under the lashes that Tom himself had once told me were "too long and black to be tidy," I saw that he was in a condition to get the full shock. "If anybody wakes up this town it will be I," I said as I flung down the gauntlet with a high head.

"Here, Molly, here are the keys of my

office, and the spark-plug to the Hup; you can cut off a lock of my hair, and if Judy has got a cake I'll eat it out of your hands. Shall it be California or Nova Scotia? And I prefer *my* bride served in light gray tweed." Tom really is adorable and I let him snuggle up just one cousinly second, then we both laughed and began to plan what Tom was horrible enough to call the resurrection razoo. But I kept that delicious rose-embroidered treasure all to myself. I wanted him to meet it entirely unprepared.

I was glad we had both got over our excitement and were sitting decorously at several inches' distance apart when the judge drew the grays up to the gate and we both went down to the sidewalk to ask him and the lovely long lady to come in. They couldn't; but we stood and talked to them long enough for Mrs.

Johnson to get a good look at us from across the street and I was afraid I would find Aunt Adeline in a faint when I went into the house.

Miss Chester was delightfully gracious about the dinner—I almost called it the début dinner—and the expression on the judge's face when he accepted! I was glad she was sitting sidewise to him and couldn't see. Some women like to make other women unhappy, but I think it is best for you to keep them blissfully unconscious until you get what you want. Anyway, I like that girl all over and I can't see that her neck is so absolutely impossibly flowery. However, I think she might have been a little more considerate about discussing Alfred's London triumph over the Italian mission. As a punishment I let Tom put his arm around my waist as we stood watching them drive off and then was sorry for the left gray horse that shied and came in for a crack of the judge's irritated whip.

Then I refused to let Tom come inside the gate and he went down the street whistling, only when he got to the purple lilac he turned and kissed his hand to me. That, Mrs. Johnson just couldn't stand and she came across the street immediately and called me back to the gate.

"You are tempting Providence, Molly Carter," she exclaimed decidedly. "Don't you know Tom Pollard is nothing but a fly-up-the-creek? As a husband he'd chew the rope and run away like a puppy the first time your back was turned. Besides being your cousin, he's younger than you. What do you mean?"

"He's just a week younger, Mrs. Johnson, and I wouldn't tie him for worlds, even if I married him," I said meekly.

Somehow I like Mrs. Johnson enough to be meek with her and it always brings her to a higher point of excitement.

"Tie, nonsense; marrying is roping in with ball and chain, to my mind. And a week between a man and a woman in their cradles gets to be fifteen years between them and their graves. I'm going to make you the subject of a silent prayer at the next missionary meeting, and I must go home now to see that Sally cooks up a few of Mr. Johnson's crotchets for supper." And she began to hurry away.

"I don't believe you'll be able to make it a 'silent' session about me, Mrs. Johnson," I called after her, and she laughed back from her own front gate. Marriage is the only worm in the bud of Mrs. Johnson's life, and her laugh has a snap to it even if it is not very sugary sweet.

When I told Judy about the dinner-party and asked her to get the yellow barber to come help her and her nephew wait on the table she grinned such a wide grin that I was afraid of being swallowed. She understood that Aunt Adeline wouldn't be interested in it until I had time to tell her all about it. Anyway, she will be going over to Springfield on a pilgrimage to see Mr. Henderson's sister next week. She doesn't know it yet; but I do.

After that I spent all the rest of the evening in planning my dinner-party and I had a most royal good time. I always have had lots of company, but mostly the spend-the-day kind with relatives, or more relatives to supper. That's what most entertaining in Hillsboro is like, but, as I say, once in a while the old slow pacer wakes up.

I'll never forget my first real dinner-party, as the flower girl for Caroline

Evans' wedding, when she married the Chicago millionaire, from which Hillsboro has never yet recovered. I was sixteen, felt dreadfully naked without a tucker in my dress, and saw Alfred for the first time in evening clothes—his first. I can hardly stand thinking about how he looked even now. I haven't been to very many dinner-parties in my life, but from this time on I mean to indulge in them often. Candle-light, pretty women's shoulders, black coat sleeves, cut glass and flowers are good ingredients for a joy-drink, and why not?

But when I got to planning about the gorgeous food I wanted to give them all, I got into what I feel came near being a serious trouble. It was writing down the recipe for the nesselrode pudding they make in my family that undid me. Suddenly hunger rose up from nowhere and gripped me by the throat, gnawed me all over like a bone, then shook me until I was limp and unresisting. I must have astralized myself down to the pantry, for when I became conscious I found myself in company with a loaf of bread, a plate of butter and a huge jar of jam.

I sat down by the long table by the window and slowly prepared to enjoy myself. I cut off four slices and buttered them to an equal thickness and then more slowly put a long silver spoon into the jam. I even paused to admire in Judy's mirror over the table the effect of the cascade of lace that fell across my arm and lost itself in the blue shimmer of old Rene's masterpiece of a negligée, then deep down I buried the spoon in the purple sweetness. I had just lifted it high in the air when out of the lilac-scented dark of the garden came a laugh.

"Why, Molly, Molly, Molly!" drawled that miserable man-doctor as he came and leaned on the sill right close to my elbow. The spoon crashed on the table and I turned and crashed into words.

"You are cruel, cruel, John Moore, and I hate you worse than I ever did before, if that is possible. I'm hungry, hungry to death, and now you've spoiled it all! Go away before I wet this nice crisp bread and jam with tears into a mush I'll have to eat with a spoon. You don't know what it is to want something sweet so bad you are willing to steal it—from yourself!" I fairly blazed my eyes down into his and moved as far away from him as the table would let me.

"Don't I, Molly?" he asked softly, after looking straight in my eyes for a long minute that made me drop my head until the blue bow I had tied on the end of my

"My Molly, Molly, Molly!"

long plait almost got into the scattered jam. Even at such a moment as that I felt how glad old Rene would have been to have given such a nice man as the doctor a treat like that blue silk chef-d'œuvre of hers. I was glad myself.

"Don't I, Peaches?" he asked again in a still softer voice. Again I had that sensation of being against something warm and great and good like your own mother's breast and I don't know how I controlled it enough not to—to—

"Well, have some jam then," I managed to say with a little laugh as I turned away and picked up the silver spoon.

"Thank you, I will, all of it and the bread and butter, too," he answered, in that detestable friendly tone of voice as he drew himself up and sat in the window. "Hustle, Peaches, if you are going to feed me, for I'm ravenous. It took

Sam Benson's wife the longest time to have the shortest baby I ever experienced and I haven't had any supper. You have; so I don't mind taking it all away from you."

"Supper," I sniffed as I spread the jam on those lovely, lovely slices of bread and thick butter that I had fixed for my own self. "That apple-toast combination tires me so now that I forget it if I can." As I handed him the first slice of drippy lusciousness I turned my head away. He thought it was from the expression of that jam, but it was from his eyes.

"Slice up the whole loaf, Peaches, and let's get on a jam jag! Come with me just this once and forget—forget—" He didn't finish his sentence and I'm glad. We neither of us said anything more as I fed him that whole loaf. I found that the bite I took off of each piece I had ready for him when he finished with the one he had in hand satisfied me as nothing I had ever eaten in all my life before had done, while at the same time my nibbles soothed his conscience about robbing me.

His teeth are big and strong and white and his jaws work like machinery. He is the strongest man I ever saw, and his gauntness is all muscle. What is that glow a woman gets from feeding a hungry man whom she likes with her own hands; and why should I want to be certain that he kissed the lace on my sleeve as it brushed his face when I reached across him to catch an inquisitive rose that I saw peeping in the window at us?

LEAF FIFTH

BLUE ABSINTHE

"THE juice of a lemon in two glasses of cold water, to be drunk immediately on wakening!" Page eleven! I've handed myself that lemon every morning now until I am sensitive with myself about it. If there was ever anybody "on the water wagon" it's I, and I have to sit on the front seat from dawn to dusk to get in the gallon of water I'm supposed to consume in that time. Sometime I'm going to get mixed up and try to drink my bath if I don't look out. I dreamed night before last that I was taking a bath in a glass of ice-cream soda-water and trying to hide from Doctor John behind the dab of ice-cream that seemed inadequate for food or protection. I haven't had even one glass for two months and I woke up in a cold perspiration of embarrassment and raging hunger.

I don't know what I'm going to do about this book and I've got myself into trouble about writing things besides records in it. He looked at me this morning as coolly as if I was just anybody and said:

"I would like to see that record now, Mrs. Molly. It seems to me you are about as slim as you want to be. How did you tip the scales last time you weighed, and have you noticed any trouble at all with your heart?"

"I weigh one hundred and thirty-four pounds and I've got to melt and freeze and starve off that four," I answered, ignoring the heart question and also the question of producing this book. Wonder what he would do if I gave it to him to read just as it is?

"How about the heart?" he persisted, and I may have imagined the smile in his eyes for his mouth was purely professional. Anyway, I lowered my lashes down on to my cheeks and answered experimentally:

"Sometimes it hurts." Then a cyclone happened to me.

"Come here to me a minute!" he said quickly and he turned me around and put his head down between my shoulders and held me so tight against his ear that I could hardly breathe.

"Expand your chest three times and breathe as deep as you can," he ordered from against by back buttons. I expanded and breathed—pretty quickly at that.

"Breathe as deep as you can"

"Now hold your breath as long as you can," he commanded, and it fitted my mood exactly to do so.

"Can't find anything," he said at last, letting me go and looking carefully at my face. His eyes were all anxiety; and I liked it. "When does it hurt you and how?" he asked anxiously.

"Moonlight nights and lonesomely," I answered before I could stop myself, and what happened then was worse than any cyclone. He got white for a minute and just looked at me as if I was a bug stuck on a pin, then gave a short little laugh and turned to the table.

"I didn't understand you were joking," he said quietly.

That maddened me and I would have done anything to make him think I was not the foolish thing he evidently had classified me as being. I snatched at my mind and shook out a mixture of truth and lies that fooled even myself and gave them to him, looking straight in his face. I would have cracked all the ten commandments to save myself from his contempt.

"I'm not joking," I said jerkily; "I *am* lonesome. And worse than being lonesome, I'm scared. I ought to have stayed just the quiet relict of Mr. Carter and gone on to church meetings with Aunt Adeline and let myself be fat and respectable; but I haven't got the character. You thought I went to town to buy a monument, and I didn't; I bought enough clothes for two brides, and now I'm scared to wear 'em, and I don't know what you'll think when you see my bankbook. Everybody is talking about me and that dinner-party Tuesday night, and Aunt Adeline says she can't live in a house of mourning so desecrated any longer; she's going back to the cottage. Aunt Bettie Pollard says that if I want to get married I ought to do it to Mr. Wilson Graves because of the seven children and then everybody would be so relieved that they are taken care of that they would forget that Mr. Carter hasn't been dead quite one year yet. Mrs. Johnson says I ought to be declared a minor and put as a ward to you. I can't help Judge Wade's sending me flowers and Tom's sitting on my front steps night and day. I'm not strong enough to carry him away and murder him. I am perfectly miserable and I'm—"

"Now that'll do, Molly, just hush for a half-minute and let me talk to you," said Doctor John as he took my hand in his and drew me near him. "No wonder your heart hurts if it has got all that load

of trouble on it and we'll just get a little
of that 'scare' off. You put yourself in
my hands and you are to do just as I tell
you, and I say—forget it! Come with
me while I make a call. It is a long drive
and I'm—I'm lonesome sometimes myself."

I saw the worst was over and I
breathed freely again, but I had talked so
much truth in that fiction that I felt just
as I said I did, which is a slightly un-
natural feeling for a woman. There was
nothing for it but to go with him, and
I wanted to most awfully.

To my dying day I'll never forget that
little house, way out on the Cane Run
Pike, he took me to in his shabby little
car. Just two tiny rooms, but they were
clean and quiet and a girl with the sweet-
est face I ever saw lay in the bed with her
eyes bright with pride and a tiny, tiny

little bundle close beside her. The young farmer was red with embarrassment and anxiety.

"She's all right to-day, but she worries because she don't think I can tend to the baby right," he said; and he did look helpless. "Her mother had to go home for two days, but is coming to-morrow. I dasn't undress and wash the youngster myself. It won't hurt him to stay bundled up until granny comes, will it, Doc?"

"Not a bit," answered Doctor John in his big comforting voice.

But I looked at the girl and I understood her. She wanted that baby clean and fresh even if it was just five days old, and I felt all of a sudden terribly capable. I picked up the bundle and went into the other room with it where a kettle was boiling on the stove and a large bucket by the door. I found things by just a glance from her, and the hour I spent with that small baby was one of the most delicious of all my life. I never was left entirely to myself with one before and I did all I wanted to this one, guided by instinct and desire. He slept right through and was the darlingest thing I ever saw when I laid him back on the bed by her. I never looked in Doctor John's direction once, though I felt him all the time.

But on the way home I gave myself the surprise of my life! Suddenly I turned my face against his sleeve and cried as I never had before. I felt safe, for it is a cliff road and he had to drive carefully. However, he managed to press that one arm against my cheek in a way that comforted me into stopping when I saw we were near town. I got out of the car at the garage and walked away through the garden home without looking in his direction at all. I never seem to be able to look at him as I do at other people. We hadn't spoken two words since we had left the little house in the woods with that happy-faced girl in it. He has more sense than just a man.

It was almost dusk and I stopped in the garden a minute to pull the dirt closer around some of the bachelor's-buttons that had "popped" the ground some weeks ago. Thinking about them made me regain my spirits and I went on in the house to be scolded for whatever Aunt Adeline had thought up while I was gone to do it to me about. Judy told me with her broadest grin that she had gone down to her sister-in-law's for supper and I sat down on the steps with a sigh of relief.

Some days are like tin cocoanut graters

that everybody uses to grate you against and this was one for me. For an hour I sat and grated my own self against Alfred's letter that had come in the morning. I realized that I would just have to come to some sort of decision about what I was going to do, for he wrote that he was to sail in a day or two, and ships do travel so fast these days.

I love him and always have, of that I am sure. He offers me the most wonderful life in the world and no woman could help being proud to accept it. I am lonely, more lonely than I was even willing to confess to Doctor John. I can't go on living this way any longer. Ruth Chester has made me see that if I want Alfred it will be now or never and—quick. I know now that she loves him, and she ought to have her show if I don't want him. The way she idolizes and idealizes him is a marvel of womanly stupidity.

Some women like to collect men's hearts and hide them away from other women on cold storage and the helpless things can't help themselves.

I have contempt for that sort of butcher, and I love Ruth!

It's my duty to look the matter in the face before I look in Alfred's—and *decide*. If not Alfred, what then?

First—no husband. That's out of the question! I'm not strong-minded enough to crank my own motor-car and study woman's suffrage. I prefer to suffer at the hands of some cruel man and trust to beguiling him into doing just as I say. I like men, can't help it, and want one for my own. I don't count poor Mr. Carter.

Second—if not Alfred, who? Judge

Wade is so delightful that I flutter at the thought, but his mother is Aunt Adeline's own best friend and they have ideas in common. She is so religious that living with her would be like having the sacrament for daily bread. Still, living with him might have adventures. I never saw such eyes! The girl he wanted to marry died of tuberculosis and he wears a locket with her in it yet. I'd like to reward him for such faithfulness with a nice husky wife to wear instead of the locket. But then Alfred's been faithful too! I look at Ruth Chester and realize how faithful, and my heart melts to him in my breast—my hips have almost all melted away, too, so I had better keep the heart cold enough to handle if I want anything left at all for him to come home to.

BLUE ABSINTHE

In some ways Tom Pollard is the most congenial man I ever knew. You have to say "don't" to him all the time, but what woman doesn't like a little impertinence once in a while? I flavor all Tom's dare-devil kisses with kinship when I feed them to my conscience, and I truly try to make him be serious about the important things in life like going to church with his mother and working all day, even if he is rich. I wish he wasn't so near kin to me! Now, there, I feel in Ruth Chester's way again! One of the things that keeps the devil so busy is taking helpless widows to the heights of knowledge and showing them kingdoms of men that girls never dream even exist. If all women could have been born with widow-eyes, things would run much more smoothly along the marriage and giving-in-marriage line. And the poor men are most of them as ignorant as girls about what to do.

I suppose I really would be doing a righteous thing to marry Mr. Graves, and I would adore all those children to start with, but I know Billy wouldn't get on with them at all. I can't even consider it on his account, but I'll let the nice old chap come on for a few times more to see me, for he really is interesting and we have suffered things in common. Mrs. Graves lacked the kind of temperament poor Mr. Carter did. I'd like to make it all up to him, but if Billy wouldn't be happy, that settles it, and I don't know how good his boys are. I couldn't have Billy corrupted.

And so, as there is nobody else exactly suitable in town, it all simmers down to one or the other of these or Alfred. In my heart I knew that I couldn't hesitate a minute—and in the flash of a second I *decided*. Of course I love Alfred and I'll take him gladly and be the wife he has waited for all these six lonely years. I'll make everything up to him if I have to diet to keep thin for him the rest of my life. I likely will have that very thing to do and I get weak at the idea. Before I burn this book I'll have to copy it all out and be chained to it for life. At the thought my heart dropped like a sinker to my toes; but I hauled it up to its normal place with picturing to myself how Alfred would look when he saw me in that old blue muslin done over into a Rene wonder. However, old heart would show a strange propensity for sinking down into my slippers without any reason at all. Tears were even coming into my eyes when Tom suddenly came over the fence and picked me and the heart up together and put us into an adventure of the first water.

"Molly," he said in the most nonchalant manner imaginable, "we've got a dandy, strolling, gipsy band up at the hotel; the dining-room floor is all waxed and I'm asking for the first dance with the young and radiant Mrs. Carter. Get into a glad rag and don't keep me waiting."

"Tom," I gasped!

"Oh, be a sport, Moll, and don't take water! You said you would wake up this town, and now do it. It seems twenty instead of six years since I had my arms around you to music and I'm not going to wait any longer. Everybody is there and they can't all dance with Miss Chester."

That settled it—I couldn't let a visiting girl be danced to death. Of course I had planned to make a dignified début under

my own roof, backed up by the presence
of ancestral and marital rosewood, silver
and mahogany, as a widow should, but
duty called me to de-weed myself amidst
the informality of an impromptu dance
at the little town hotel. And in the fifteen
minutes Tom gave me I de-weeded to
some purpose and flowered out to still
more. I never do anything by halves.

In that—that—trousseau old Rene had
made me there was one, what she called
"simple" lingerie frock. And it looked
just as simple as the check it called for,
a one and two ciphers back of it. It was
of linen as sheer as a cobweb, real lace
and tiny delicious incrustations of embroidery. It fitted in lines that melted
into curves, had enticements in the shape
of a long sash and a dangerous breast-
knot of shimmery blue, the color of my
eyes, and I looked new-born in it.

I'm glad that poor Mr. Carter was so stern with me about rats and things in my hair, now that they are out of style, for I've got lots of my own left in consequence of not wearing other peoples'. It clings and coils to my head just any old way that looks as if I had spent an hour on it. That made me able to be ready to go down to Tom in only ten minutes over the time he gave me.

I stopped on next to the bottom step in the wide old hall and called Tom to turn out the light for me, as Judy had gone.

I have turned out that light lots of times, but I felt it best to let Tom see me in a full light when we were alone. It is well I did! At first it stunned him,— and it is a compliment to any woman to stun Tom Pollard. But Tom doesn't stay stunned long and I only succeeded in suppressing him after he had landed two kisses on my shoulder, one on my hair and one on the back of my neck.

"Molly," he said, standing off and looking at me with shining eyes, "you are one lovely dream. Your shoulders are flushed velvet, your cheeks are peaches under cream, your eyes are blue absinthe and your mouth a red devil. Come on before I get drunk looking at you." I didn't know whether I liked that or not and turned down the light quickly myself and went to the gate hurriedly. Tom laughed and behaved himself.

Everybody in town was up to the hotel and everybody was nice to me, girls and all. There is a bunch of lovely posy girls in this town and they were all in full flower. Most of the men were college boys home for vacation, and while they are a few years younger than me, I have been friends with them for always and they know how I dance. I didn't even get near enough to the wall to know it was there, though I was conscious of Aunt Bettie and Mrs. Johnson sitting on it at one end of the room, and every time I passed them I flirted with them until I won a smile from them both. I wish I could be sure of hearing Mrs. Johnson tell Aunt Adeline all about it.

And it was well I did come to save Ruth Chester from a dancing death, for she is as light as a feather and sails on the air like thistle-down. I felt sorry for Tom, for when he danced with me he could see her, and when he danced with her I pouted at him, even over Judge Wade's arm. I verily believe it was from being really rattled that he asked little Pet Buford to dance with him—by mistake as it were. After that if Pet breathed a single strain of music out of

"Molly, you are one lovely dream"

his arms I didn't see it. I knew that gone expression on his face and it made me feel so lonesome that I was more gracious to the judge than was exactly safe. He dances just as magnificently as he exists in life and it is a kind of ceremonial to do it with him. The boys all wore white flannels, and most of the men, but the judge was as formally dressed as he would have been in mid-winter, and I wondered if Alfred could be half as distinguished to look at. I suppose my eyes must have been telling on me about how grand I thought he was looking because he—well, I was rather relieved when one of the boys took me out of his arms for a good, long, swinging two-step.

And how I did enjoy it all, every single minute of it! My heart beat time to the music as if it would never tire of doing so. Miss Chester and I exchanged little laughs and scraps of conversation in between times and I fell deeper and deeper in love with her. Every pound I have melted and frozen and starved off me has brought me nearer to her and I just *can't* think about how I am going to hurt her in a few days now. I put the thought from me and so let myself swing out into thoughtlessness with one of the boys. And after that I really didn't know with whom I was dancing, I began to get so intoxicated with it all.

I never heard musicians play better or get more of the spirit of dance in their music than those did to-night. They had just given us the most lovely swinging things, one after another, when suddenly they all stopped and the leader drew his bow across his violin. Never in all my life have I ever heard anything like the call of that waltz from that gipsy's strings. It laughed you a signal and you felt yourself follow the first strain.

Just then somebody happened to take me from whomever I was with and I caught step and glided off the universe. The strongest arms that I had felt that evening—or ever—held me and I didn't have to look up to see who it was. I don't know why I knew but I did. I wasn't clasped so very close to him or left to float by myself an inch; I was just a part of him like the arms themselves or the hand that mine molded into. And while that wonder-music teased and cajoled and mocked and rocked and sobbed and throbbed, I laid my cheek against his coat sleeve and gave myself away, I didn't care to whom.

Again that strange sense of some wonderful eternal good came to me and I found myself humming Billy's little "soul to keep" prayer against the doctor's sleeve to the tune of that magic waltz. I had never danced with him before, of course, but I felt as if I had been doing it always, and I melted in his arms as that baby had wilted to his mother out in the cabin a few hours earlier and I don't see how such happiness as that *could* stop. But with a soft entreating wail the music came to an end and there the doctor was, smiling down into my face with his whimsical friendly smile that woke me up all over.

"Somebody has stolen a rose from the Carter garden and brought it to the dance," he said with a laugh that was for me alone.

"No," I flashed back, "a string-bean." And with that I danced off again with the judge, while the doctor disappeared through the door, and I heard the chuck of his car as it whirled away. He had just stopped in for a second to see the fun and God had given me that gipsy waltz with him, because He knew I needed something like that in my life to keep for always.

This has been a happy night, in which I betrothed myself to Alfred, though he doesn't know it yet. I am going to take it as a sign that life for us is going to be brilliant and gay and full of laughter and love.

I haven't had Billy in my arms to-day and I don't know how I shall ever get myself to sleep if I let myself think about it. His sleep-place on my breast aches. It is a comfort to think that the great big God understands the women folk that He makes, even if they don't understand themselves.

LEAF SIXTH

THE RESURRECTION RAZOO

MOST parties are just bunches of
selfish people who go off in the
corners and have good times all by themselves, but in Hillsboro, Tennessee, it is
not that way. Everybody that is not invited helps the hostess get ready and have
nice things for the others, and sometimes
I think they really have the best time of
all.

This morning Aunt Bettie came up my
front steps before breakfast with a large
basketful of things for my dinner and I
wondered what I would have collected
to be served to those people by the time
all my neighbors had made their prize

contributions. It took Aunt Bettie and Judy a half-hour to unpack her things and set them in the refrigerator and on the pantry shelves. One was a plump fruit-cake that had been keeping company in a tight box with a sponge soaked in sherry for ever since New Year's. It was ripe, or smelled so. It made me gnaw under my belt.

A little later Judy was exclaiming over a two-year-old ham that had been simmered in port and larded with egg dressing, when Mrs. Johnson came in and began to unpack her basket, which was mostly bottles of things she said she used to "stick" food. The ginger-colored barber got the run of them before the dinner was over and got badly stuck, so Judy says. That's what made him make the mistake.

I had planned to have a lot of strange

127

food and had ordered some things up from a caterer in the city, but I telephoned the express man not to deliver them until the next day, even if they did spoil. How could I use soft shelled crabs when Mrs. Wade had sent me word that she was going to bake some brook trout by a recipe of the judge's grandmother's? Mrs. Hampton Buford had let me know about two fat little summer turkeys she was going to stuff with corn-pone and green sage, and *fillet mignon* seemed foolish eating beside them. But when the little bit of a baby pig, roasted whole with an apple in its mouth, looking too frisky and innocent for worlds with his little baked tail curled up in the air, arrived from Mrs. Caruthers Cain, I went out into the garden and laughed at the idea of having spent money for lobsters, to be shipped alive and to be served broiled in their own shells.

When I got back in the kitchen things were well under way, everything smelling grand, and Aunt Bettie in full swing matching up my dinner guests.

"Nobody in this town could suit me better than Pet Buford for a daughter-in-law and I believe I'll have all the east rooms done over in blue chintz for her. I think that would be the best thing to set off her blue eyes and corn silk hair," she was saying as she cut orange peel into strips.

"You've planned the refurnishing of that east wing to suit the style of nearly every girl in Hillsboro since Tom put on long trousers, Bettie Pollard, and they are just as they have been for fifteen years since you did over the whole house," said Mrs. Johnson as she poured a wine-glass half full from one bottle and added a tablespoonful from another.

"Well, I think he is really interested now from the way he danced most of his time with her down at the hotel the other night, and I have hopes I never had before. Now, Molly, do put him between you and her, sort of cornered, so he can't even *see* Ruth Chester. She is too old for him." And Tom's mother looked at me over the orange peel as to a confederate.

"Humph, I'd like to see you or Molly or any woman 'corner' Tom Pollard," said Mrs. Johnson with a wry smile as she tasted the concoction in the wine-glass.

"I have to put him at the end of the table because he is my kinsman and the only host I've got at present, Aunt Bettie," I said regretfully. I always take every chance to rub in Tom's and my relationship on Aunt Bettie, so she won't notice our flirtation.

"I'd put John Moore at the head of the table if I were you, Molly Carter, because he's about the only man you've invited that has got any sense left since you and that Chester girl took to visiting Hillsboro. He's a host of steadiness in himself and the way he ignores all you women, who would run after him if he would let you, shows what he is. He has my full confidence," and as she delivered herself of this judgment of Doctor John, Mrs. Johnson drove in all the corks tight and began to pound spice.

"He's not out of the widower-woods yet, Caroline," said Aunt Bettie with her most speculative smile. "I have about decided on him for Ruth since the judge has taken to following Molly about as bad as Billy Moore does. But don't you all say a word, for John's mighty timid, and I don't believe, in spite of all these years, he's had a single notion yet. If he had had he'd have tried a set-to with you, Molly, like all the rest of the shy birds in town. He doesn't see a woman as anything but a patient at the end of a spoon, and mighty kind and gentle he does the dosing of them, too. Just the other day—dearie me, Judy, what has boiled over now?" And in the excitement that ensued I escaped to the garden.

Yes, Aunt Bettie is right about Doctor John; he doesn't see a woman, and there is no way to make him. What she had said about it made me realize that he had always been like that, and I told myself that there was no reason in the world why my heart should beat in my slippers

on that account. Still I don't see why
Ruth Chester should have her head literally thrown against that stone wall and
I wish Aunt Bettie wouldn't. It seemed
like a desecration even to try to match-
make him and it made me hot with indig-
nation all over. I dug so fiercely at the
roots of my phlox with a trowel I had
picked up that they groaned so loud I
could almost hear them. I felt as if I
must operate on something. And it was
in this mood that Alfred's letter found
me.

It had a surprise in it and I sat back
on the grass and read it with my heart
beating like a trip-hammer. He had
sailed the day he had posted it and he was
due to arrive in New York almost as
soon as it did, just any hour now I cal-
culated in a flash. And "from New York
immediately to Hillsboro" he had written

in words that fairly sung themselves off the paper. I was frightened—so frightened that the letter shook in my hands, and with only the thought of being sure that I might be alone for a few minutes with it, I fled to the garret.

Surely no woman ever in all the world read such a letter as that, and no wonder my breath almost failed me. It was a love-letter in which the cold paper was transubstantiated into a heart that beat against mine and I bowed my head over it as I wet it with tears. I knew then that I had taken his coming back lightly; had fussed over it and been silly-proud of it; while not *really* caring at all. All that awful melting away of my fatness seemed just a lack of confidence in his love for me; he wouldn't have minded if I weighed five hundred, I felt sure. He loved me—really, really, really; and I

134

had sat and weighed him with a lot of men who were nothing more than amused by my flightiness, or taken with my beauty, and who wouldn't have known such love if it were shown to them through a telescope.

I reached into a trunk that stood right beside me and took out a box that I hadn't looked into for years. His letters were all there and his photographs that were as handsome as the young god of love himself. I could hardly see them through my tears, but I knew that they were dim in places with being cried over when I had put them away years ago after Aunt Adeline decided that I was to be married. I kissed the poor little-girl cry-spots; and with that a perfect flood of tears rose to my eyes—but they didn't fall, for there, right in front of me, stood a more woe-stricken human being than

I could possibly be, if I judged by appearances.

"Molly, Molly," gulped Billy, "I am so sick I'm going to die here on the floor," and he sank into my arms.

"Oh, Billy, what is the matter?" I gasped and gave him a little terrified shake.

"Mamie Johnson did it—poked her finger down her throat and mine, too," he wailed against my breast. "We was full of things folks gived us to eat and couldn't eat no more. She said if we did that with our fingers it would all come up and we would have room for some more then. She did it and I'm going to die dead—dead!"

"No, no, lover; you'll be all right in a second. Stay quiet here in your Molly's lap and you will be well in just a few

His letters were all there and his photographs

minutes," I said with a smile I hid in his yellow mop as I kissed the drake-tail kiss-spot. "Where's Mamie?" I thought to ask with the greatest apprehension.

"In the garden eating cup-cake Judy baked hot for both of us. She didn't frow up as much as I did—or maybe more." He answered, snuggling close and much comforted.

"Don't ever, ever do that again, Billy," I said, giving him both a hug and a shake. "It's piggy to eat more than you can hold and then still want more. What would your father say?"

"Doc ain't no good and I don't care what he says," answered Billy with spirit. "He don't play no more and he don't laugh no more and he don't eat no more hardly, too. I ain't a-going to live in that house with him more'n two days longer.

I want to come over and sleep in your bed with blue ribbons on the posts and have you to play with me, Molly."

"Don't say that, lover, ever again," I said as I bent over him. "Your father is the best man in the world, and you must never, never leave him."

"I bet I will, when I get big enough to kill a bear," answered Billy decidedly. "Say, do you reckon Mamie saved even a little piece of that cake? I 'spect I had better go see," and he slipped out of my arms and was gone before I could hold him.

It *is* a lonely house across the garden with the big and the tiny man in it all by themselves! And tears, from another corner of my heart entirely, rose to my eyes at the thought, but they, too, never fell, for I heard Mrs. Johnson calling and I had to run down quick and see what new delicacy had arrived for my party.

Uncle Thomas Pollard had sent me a quart bottle of his private stock with the message to put the mint to soak just one hour and twenty minutes before the men came. I made room for it beside the case of champagne on the cellar shelf and wondered how they would stand it all. We don't have champagne often in Hillsboro, and when we do nobody seems to want to cut down on the juleps, consequently—well, nothing ever really happens! However, it must have been the champagne that made Tom act as he did. He was never like that before.

Somehow I didn't enjoy dressing tonight for my dinner as I did for the dance, and when I was through I stood before the mirror and looked at myself a long time. I was very tall and slim and

—well, I suppose I might say regal in that amethyst crêpe with the soft rose-point, but I looked to myself about the eyes as I had been doing for years when I put on my Sunday clothes to go to church with Mr. Carter. He was always in a hurry and I didn't care about looking at myself in the mirror anyway; nobody else ever looked at me and what was the use? And to-night that Rene triumph made me feel no different from one of Miss Hettie Primm's conceptions that I had been wearing for ages with indifference and total lack of style. I shrugged my shoulder almost out of the dress with what I thought was sadness, though it felt a trifle like temper, too, and went on down into the garden to see if any of my flowers had a cheer-up message for me.

But it was a bored garden I stepped into just as the last purple flush of day was being drunk down by the night. The tall white lilies laid their heads over on my breast and went to sleep before I had said a word to them, and the nasturtiums snarled around my feet until they got my slippers stained with green. Only Billy's bachelor's-button stood up stiff and sturdy, slightly flushed with imbibing the night dew, and tipped me an impertinent wink. I felt cheered at the sight of them and bent down to gather a bunch of them to wear, even if they did swear at my amethyst draperies, when an amused smile that was done out loud came from the path just behind me.

"Don't gather them all to-night, Mrs. Peaches," said Doctor John teasingly, as he stooped beside me. "Leave a few for —for the others." I waked up in a half-second and so did all those prying flowers, I felt sure.

141

"I was just gathering them for place bouquets for—for the girls," I said stupidly as I moved over a little nearer to him. Why it is that the minute that man comes near me I get warm and comfortable and stupid, and as young as Billy, and bubbly and sad and happy and cross is more than I can say, but I do. I never possibly know how to answer any remark that he may happen to make unless it is something that makes me lose my temper. His next remark was the usual spark.

"Better give them the run of the garden—alone, Mrs. Molly. No show for 'em unless you do," he said laughingly, "or the buttons' either," he added under his breath so I could just hear it. I wish Mrs. Johnson could have heard how soft his voice lingered over that little half-sentence. She is so experienced she could have told me if it meant—but of course he isn't like other men!

There are lots of questions I'm going to ask Alfred after I'm married to him— Mr. Carter didn't know anything about anything and I never cared to ask him, but I wonder how you know when—

"Oh, you Molly," came a hail in Tom's voice from the gate, just as I was making up my mind to try and think up something to wither the doctor with, and he and Ruth Chester came up the front walk to meet us. I wondered why I was having a party in my house when being alone in my garden with just a neighbor was so much more fun, but I had to begin to enjoy myself right off, for in a few minutes all the rest came.

I don't think I ever saw my house look so lovely before. Mrs. Johnson had put all the flowers out of hers and Mrs.

Cain's garden all over everything and the table was a mass of soft pink roses that were shedding perfume and nodding at one another in their most society manner. There is no glimmer in the world like that which comes from really old polished silver and rosewood and mahogany, and one's great-great-grandmother's hand-woven linen feels like oriental silk across one's knees.

Suddenly I felt very stately and grand-damey and responsible as I looked at them all across the roses and sparkling glasses. They were lovely women, all of them, and could such men be found anywhere else in the world? When I left them all to go out into the big universe to meet the distinctions that I knew my husband would have for me, would I sit at salt with people who loved me like this? I saw Pet Buford say something

144

to Tom about me that I know was lovely
from the way he smiled at me; and the
judge's eyes were a full cup for any
woman to have offered her. Then in a
flash all the love-fragrance seemed to go
to my head—Tom's mixing of that julep
had been skiiful, too—and tears rose to
my eyes, and there I might have been crying at my own party if I hadn't felt a
strong warm hand laid on mine as it
rested on my lap and Doctor John's kind
voice teased into my ears: "Steady, Mrs.
Peaches, there's the loving-cup to come
yet," he whispered. I hated him, but
held on to his thumb tight for half a
minute. He didn't know what the matter
really was, but he understood what I
needed. He always does.

And after that everybody had a good
time, the ginger barber and Judy as much
as anybody, and I could see Aunt Bettie

and Mrs. Johnson peeping in the pantry door, having the time of their lives, too.

That dinner was going like an airship on a high wind, when something happened to tangle its tail feathers and I can hardly write it for trembling yet. It was a simple little blue telegram, but it might have been nitro-glycerin on a tear for the way it acted. It was for me, but the ginger barber handed it to Tom and he opened it and, looking at me over his full —after many times emptied—glass, he solemnly read it out loud. It said:

"Landed this noon. Have I your permission to come to Hillsboro immediately? Answer. Alfred."

It was dreadful! Nobody said a word and Tom laid the telegram right down in his plate, where it immediately began to soak up the dressing of his salad. He

was so white and shaky that Pet looked
at him in amazement, and then I am sure
she had the good sense to find his hand
under the cloth and hold it, for his shoulder hovered against hers and the color
came back to his face as he smiled down
at her. I don't believe I'll ever get the
courage to look at Tom again until he
marries Pet, which he'll do now, I feel
sure.

And as for the judge and Ruth Chester, I was glad they were sitting beside
each other, for I could avoid that side of
the table with my eyes until I had steadied
myself a few seconds at least. The surprise made the others I had been dining
seem statues from the stone age, and only
Mr. Graves' fork failed to hang fire. His
appetite is as strong as his nerves and
Delia Hawes looked at his composure
with the relief plain in her eyes. Henri-

etta's smile in the judge's direction was
doubtful. But they were not all my lovers and why that awful silence?

I couldn't say a word, and I ai. sure I
don't know what I would have done if
it hadn't been for the doctor. He leaned
forward and his deep eyes came out in
their wonderful way and seemed to collect every pair of eyes at the table, even
the most astounded, as he raised his glass.
We all held our breaths and waited for
him to speak.

"No wonder we are all stricken dumb
at Mrs. Carter's telegram," he said in his
deep voice that commands everybody and
everything, even the terrors of birth and
death. "The whole town will be par-
alyzed at the news that its most distinguished citizen is only going to give them
two days to get ready to receive him. I
can see the panic the brass band will have

now getting the brass shined up, and I want to be the one to tell Mayor Pollard myself, so as to suggest to him to have at least a two-hour speech of welcome to hand out at the train. We'll make it one 'hot time' for him when he lands in the old town, and here's to him, God bless him. Every glass high!" They all drank, and I suppose it helped them. I wish I could have drained a quart, but I couldn't swallow a sip, though I did a good stunt of pretending.

The rest of this evening has paid me off for every sin I have ever committed or am ever going to commit. Tom took Pet home early and I hope they walked in the moonlight for hours. Tom is the kind of man that any pretty girl who is loving enough in the moonlight could comfort for anything. I'm not at all worried about him, but—

The hour I sat on my front steps and
talked to Judge Wade must have brought
gray hairs to my head if it was daylight
and I could see them. Ruth Chester had
said good-by with the loveliest haunted
look in her great dark eyes and I had felt
as if I had killed something that was alive
and that I hadn't killed it enough. Doctor John had been called from his coffee
to a patient and had gone with just a
friendly word of good night, and the
others had at last left the judge and me
alone—also in the moonlight, which I
wished in my heart somebody would put
out.

They say among the lawyers that it is
a good thing that Benton Wade is on the
bench, for it is no use to try a case against
him when he has the handling of a jury.
He just looks them in the face and tells
them how to vote. To-night he looked

"Every glass high"

me in the face and told me how to marry, and I'm not sure yet that I won't do as he says. Of course I'm in love with Alfred, but if he wants me he had better get me away quick before the judge makes all his arrangements. A woman loves to be courted with poems and flowers and deference, but she's mighty apt to marry the man who says, "Don't argue, but put on your bonnet and come with me." The fact that it was too late to get into the clerk's office saved me to-night, but in two days—

Oh, I'm crying, crying in my heart, which is worse than in my eyes, as I sit and look across my garden, where the cold moon is hanging low over the tall trees behind the doctor's house and his light in his room is burning warm and bright. They are right; *he* doesn't care if I am going away for ever with Alfred.

His quick toast to him and the lovely warm look he poured over poor frightened me at his side, as he drank his champagne, told me that once and for all. Still we have been so close together over his baby and I have grown so dependent on him for so many things that it cuts into me like a hot knife that he shouldn't care if he lost me—even for a neighbor. I shouldn't mind not having *any* husband if I could always live close by him and Billy like this, and if I married Judge Wade I could at least have him for a family physician. *No—I don't like that!* Of course I'm going with Alfred now that an accident has made me announce the fact to the whole town before he even knows it himself, but wherever I go that light in the room with that lonely man is going to burn in my heart. Hope it will throw a glow over Alfred!

LEAF SEVENTH

DASHED!

I DO believe God gave that wise angel
charge concerning me lest I get
dashed, but I just got dashed anyway,
and its my own fault, not the angel's. I
have suffered this day until I want to
lay my face down against the hem of His
garment and wait in the dust for Him
to pick me up. I shall never be able to do
it myself, and how He's going to do it I
can't see, but He will.

That dinner-party last night was bad
enough, but to-day's been worse. I didn't
sleep until long after daylight and then
Judy came in before eight o'clock with a
letter for me that looked like a state docu-

ment. I felt in my trembly bones that it was some sort of summons affair from Judge Wade; and it was. I looked into the first paragraph and then decided that I had better get up and dress and have a cup of coffee and a single egg before I tried to read it.

Incidental to my bath and dressing, I weighed and found that I had lost all four of those last surplus pounds and two more in three days. Those two extra pounds might be construed to prove love, but exactly on whom I was utterly unprepared to say. I didn't even enjoy the thinness, but took a kind of already-married look in my glass and tried to slip the egg past my bored lips and get myself to chew it down. It was work; and then I took up the judge's letter, which also was work and more of it.

He started in at the beginning of

everything, that is at the beginning of
the tuberculosis girl and I cried over the
pages of her as if she had been my own
sister. At the tenth page we buried her
and took up Alfred and I must say I saw
a new Alfred in the judge's bouquet-
strewn appreciation of him, but I didn't
want him as bad as I had the day before
when I read his own new and old letters,
and cried over his old photographs. I
suppose that was the result of some of
what the judge manages the juries with.
He'd be apt to use it on a woman and she
wouldn't find out about it until it was too
late to be anything but mad. Still when
he began on me at page sixteen I felt a
little better, though I didn't know myself
any better than I did Alfred when I got
to page twenty.

What I am, is just a poor foolish
woman, who has a lot more heart than

she can manage with the amount of brains she got with it at birth. I'm not any star in a rose-colored sky, and I don't want to inspire anybody; it's too much of a job. I want to be a healthy happy woman and a wife to a man who can inspire himself and manage me. I want to marry a thin man and have from five to ten thin children, and when I get to be thirty I want my husband to want me to be as fat as Aunt Bettie, but not let me. An inspiration couldn't be fat and I'm always in danger from hot muffins and chicken gravy. However, if I should undertake to be all the things Judge Wade said in that letter he wanted me to be to him, I should soon be skin and bones from mental and physical exercise. Still, he does live in Hillsboro and I won't let myself know how my heart aches at the thought of leaving my home—and other things. It's up in my throat and I seem always to be swallowing it, the last few days.

All the men who write me letters seem to get themselves wound up into a sky-rocket and then let themselves explode in the last paragraph and it always upsets my nerves. I was just about to begin to cry again over the last words of the judge when the only bright spot in the day so far suddenly happened. Pet Buford blew in with the pinkest cheeks and the brightest eyes I had seen since I looked in the mirror the night of the dance. She was in an awful hurry.

"Molly, dear," she said, with her words literally falling over themselves, "Tom says you'll give us some of your dinner left-overs to take for lunch in the Hup, for we are going way out to Wayne County to see some awfully fine tobacco

157

he has heard is there. I don't want to ask mother, for she won't let me go; and his mother, if he asked her, will begin to talk about us. Tom said come to you and you would understand and fix it quick. He said kiss you for him and tell you he said 'Come on in, the water's fine.' Isn't he a joke?" And we kissed and laughed and packed a basket, and kissed and laughed again for good-by. I felt amused and happy for a few minutes—and also deserted. It's a very good thing for a woman's conceit to find out how many of her lovers are just make-believes. I may have needed Tom's deflection.

Anyway, I don't know when I ever was so glad to see anybody as I was when Mrs. Johnson came in the front door. A woman who has proved to her own satisfaction that marriage is a failure is at times a great tonic to other women. I needed a tonic badly this morning and I got it.

"Well, from all my long experience, Molly," she said as she seated herself and began to hem a dish-towel with long steady stabs, "husbands are just stick candy in different jars. They may look a little different, but they all taste alike and you soon get tired of them. In two months you won't know the difference in being married to Al Bennett and Mr. Carter and you'll have to go on living with him maybe fifty years. Luck doesn't strike twice in the same place and you can't count on losing two husbands. Al's father was Mr. Johnson's first cousin and had more crochets and worse. He had silent spells that lasted a week and family prayers three times a day, though he got drunk twice a year for a month at a time. Al looks very much like him."

"Mrs. Johnson," I said after a minute's silence, while I had decided whether or not I had better tell her all about it. If a woman's in love with her husband you can't trust her to keep a secret, but I decided to try Mrs. Johnson. "I really am not engaged exactly to Alfred Bennett, though I suppose he thinks so by now if he has got the answer to that telegram. But—but something has made me —made me think about Judge Wade— that is he—what do you think of him, Mrs. Johnson?" I concluded in the most pitifully perplexed tone of voice.

"All alike, Molly; all as much alike as peas in a pod; all except John Moore, who's the only exception in all the male tribe I ever met! His marrying once was just accidental and must be forgiven him. She fell in love with him while he was treating her for typhoid, when his back was turned as it were, and it was God's own kindness in him that made him marry her when he found out how it was with the poor thing. There's not a woman in this town who could marry, that wouldn't marry him at the drop of his hat—but, thank goodness, that hat will never drop and I'll have one sensible man to comfort and doctor me down into my old age. Now, just look at that! Mr. Johnson's come home here in the middle of the morning and I'll have to get that old paper I hunted out of his desk for him last night. I wonder how he came to forget it!" It's funny how Mrs. Johnson always knows what Mr. Johnson wants before he knows himself and gets it before he asks for it!

As she went out the gate the postman came in and at the sight of another letter my heart again slunk off into my slippers, and my brain seemed about to back up in a corner and refuse to work. In a flash it came to me that men oughtn't to write letters to women very much—they really don't plow deep enough, they just irritate the top soil. I took this missive from Alfred, counted all the fifteen pages, put it out of sight under a book, looked out the window and saw the ginger barber coming dejectedly around to the side gate from the kitchen—I knew the scene he had had with Judy, about the bottle encounters of the night before—saw Mr. Johnson shooed off down the street by Mrs. Johnson; saw the doctor's car go chucking hurriedly in the garage and then my spirit turned itself to the wall and refused to be comforted. I tried my best, but failed to respond to my own remonstrances with myself, and tears were slowly gathering in a cloud of gloom

when a blue gingham, rompers-clad sun-
beam burst into the room.

"Git your night-gown and your tooth-
bresh quick, Molly, if you want to pack
'em in my trunk!" he exclaimed with his
eyes dancing and a curl standing straight
up on the top of his head, as it has a habit
of doing when he is most excited. "You
can't take nothing but them 'cause I'm
going to put in a rope to tie the whale
with when I ketch him, and it'll take up
all the rest of the room. Git 'em quick!"

"Yes, lover, I'll get them for you, but
tell Molly where it is you are going to
sail off with her in that trunk of yours?"
I asked, dropping into the game as I have
always done with him, no matter what
game of my own pressed when he called.

"On the ocean where the boats go
'cross and run right over a whale. Don't
you remember you showed me them pic-

tures of spout whales in a book, Molly?
Doc says they comes right up by the ship
and you can hear 'em shoot water and
maybe a iceberg, too. Which do you
want to ketch most, Molly, a iceberg or a
whale?" His eager eyes demanded in-
stant decision on my part of the nature
of capture I preferred. My mind quickly
reverted to those two ponderous and intense epistles I had got within the hour
and I lay back in my chair and laughed
until I felt almost merry.

"The iceberg, Billy, every time," I said
at last. "I just can't manage whales,
especially if they are ardent, which word
means hot. I like *icebergs,* or I think I
should if I could catch one."

"I don't believe you could, Molly, but
maybe Doc will let you put a rope and a
long hook in his trunk to try with if your
clothes go into mine. His is a heap the

biggest anyway and Nurse Tilly said he oughter put my things in his, but I cried and then he went up-stairs and got out that little one for me. Come see 'em!"

"What do you mean, Billy?" I asked, while a sudden fear shot all over me like lightning. "You're just playing go-away, aren't you?"

"No, I ain't playing, Molly!" he exclaimed excitedly. "Me and you and Doc is a-going across the ocean for a long, long time away from here. Doc ast me about it this morning and I told him all right and you could come with us, if you was good. He said couldn't I go without you if you was busy and couldn't come and I told him you would put things down and come if I said so. Won't you, Molly? It won't be no fun without you and you'd cry all by yourself with me gone." His little face was all drawn up with anxiety and sympathy at my lonely estate with him out of it and a cry rose up from my heart with a kind of primitive savagery at what I felt was coming down upon me.

Without waiting to take him with me, or think, or do anything but feel deadly savage anger, I hurried across the garden and into Doctor Moore's office, where he was just laying off his gloves and dust coat.

"What do you mean, John Moore, by daring, daring to think you can go and take Billy away from me?" I demanded looking at him with what must have been such fear and madness in my face that he was startled as he came close to the table against which I leaned. His face had grown white and quiet at my attack and he waited to answer for a long horrible minute that pulled me apart like one of those inquisition machines they used to torture women with when they didn't know any better modern way to do it.

"I didn't know Bill would tell you so soon, Mrs. Molly," he said at last gently, looking past me out of the window into the garden. "I was coming over just as soon as I got back from this call to talk with you about it, even if it did seem to intrude Bill's and my affairs into a day that—that ought to be all yours to be— be happy in. But Bill, you see, is no re-specter of—of other people's happy days if he wants them in his."

"Billy's happy days are mine and mine are his and he has the heart not to leave me out even if you would have him!" I exclaimed, a sob gathering in my heart at the thought that my little lover hadn't even taken in a situation that would sepa-rate him from me across an ocean.

"Bill is too young to understand when he is—is being bereaved, Molly," he said and still he didn't look at me. "I have been appointed a delegate to represent the State Medical Association at the Centennial Congress in London the middle of next month—and somehow I—feel a bit pulled lately and I thought I would take the little chap and have—have a *wanderjahr*. You won't need him now, Mrs. Peaches, and I couldn't go without him, could I?" The sadness in his voice would have killed me if I hadn't let it madden me instead.

"Won't need Billy any more!" I exclaimed with a rage that made my voice literally scorch past my lips. "Was there ever a minute in his life that I haven't needed Billy? How dare you say such a thing to me? You are cruel, cruel, and I have always known it, cold and cruel

168

like all other men who don't care how they wring the life blood out of women's hearts and are willing to use their children to do it with. Even the law doesn't help us poor helpless creatures and you can take our children and go with them to the ends of the earth and leave us suffering. I have gone on and believed that you were not like what the women say all men are and that you cared whether you hurt people or not, but now I see that you are just the same and you'll take my baby away if you want to—and I can do nothing to prevent it—nothing in the wide world—I am completely and absolutely helpless—you coward, you!"

When that awful word, the worst word that a woman can use to a man, left my lips, a flame shot up into his eyes that I thought would burn me up, but in a half-second it was extinguished by the stran-

gest thing in the world—for the situation
—a perfect flood of mirth. He sat down
in his chair and shook all over with his
head in his hands until I saw tears creep
through his fingers. I had calmed down
so suddenly that I was about to begin to
cry in good earnest when he wiped his
eyes and said with a low laugh in his
throat:

"The case is yours, Molly, settled out
of court, and the 'possession-nine-points-
of-the-law clause' works in some cases for
a woman against a man. Generally speaking, anyway, the pup belongs to the man
who can whistle him down and you can
whistle Bill from me any day. I'm just
his father and what I think or want
doesn't matter. You had better take him
and keep him!"

"I intend to." I answered haughtily,
uncertain as to whether I had better give

in and be agreeable or stay prepared to cry in case there was further argument. But suddenly a strange diffidence came into his eyes and he looked away from me as he said in queer hesitating words:

"You see, Mrs. Molly, I thought from now on your life wouldn't have exactly a place for Bill. Have you considered that you have trained him to demand you all the time and all of you? How would you manage Bill—and—and other claims?"

And if there is a contagious thing in this world it is embarrassment. I never felt anything worse in all my life than the shame that swept over me in a great hot wave when that look came into his eyes and made me realize just exactly what I had been saying to him, about what, and how I had said it. I stood perfectly still, shook all over like a leaf, and

171

wondered if I would ever be able to raise my eyes from the ground. A dizzy nauseated feeling for myself rose up in me against myself and I was just about to turn on my heels and leave him, I hoped for ever, when he came over and laid his hand on my shoulder.

"Molly," he said in a voice that might have come down from heaven on dove wings, "you can't for a moment feel or think that I don't realize and appreciate what you have been to the motherless little chap, and for life I am yours at command, as he is. I really thought it would be a relief to you to have him taken away from you for just a little while right now, and I still think it is best; but not unless you consent. You shall have him back whenever you are ready for him, and at all times both he and I are at your service to the whole of our kingdoms. Just think the matter over, won't you, and decide what you want me to do?"

Something in me died for ever, I think, when he spoke to me like that. He's not like other men and there aren't any other men on earth but him! All the rest are just bugs or bats or something worse. And I'm not anything myself. There's no excuse for my living and I wish I wasn't so healthy and likely to go on doing it. It was all over and there was nothing left for me to live for, and before I could stop myself I buried my face in my hands.

"Billy asked me to go with him on this awful whale hunt!" I sobbed out to comfort myself with the thought that somebody did care for me, regardless of just how I was further embarrassing and complicating myself in the affairs of the two men I had thought I owned and was now finding out that I had to give up. I wish I had been looking at him, for I felt him start, but he said in his big friendly voice that is so much—and never enough for me.

"Well, why not you and Al come along and make it a family party, if that is what suits Bill, the boss?"

If men would just buy good, sharp, kitchen knives and cut out women's hearts in a businesslike way it would be so much kinder of them. Why do they prefer to use dull weapons that mash the life out slowly? Everything is at an end for me to-night and that blow did it. It was a horrible cruel thing for him to say to me! I know now that I have been in love with John Moore for longer than my honor lets me admit and that I'll never love anybody else, and that also I have offered myself to him served up in every

174

known enticement and have had to be refused at least twice a day for a year. A widow can't say she didn't understand what she was doing, even to herself, but— My humiliation is complete and the only thing that can make me ever hold up my head is to puzzle him by—by *happily* marrying Alfred Bennett—and quick!

Of course, he must suspect how I feel about him, for two people couldn't both be so ignorant as not to see such an enormous thing as my love for him is, and I was the blind one. But he must never, never know that I ever realized it, for he is so good that it would distress him. I must just go on in my foolish way with him until I can get away. I'll tell him I'm sorry I was so indignant to-night and say that I think it will be fine for him to take my Billy away from me with him. I must smile at the idea of having my very soul amputated, insist that it is the only thing to do, and pack up the little soul in a steamer trunk with the smile. Just smile, that is all! Life demands smiles from a woman even if she must crush their perfume from her own heart; and she generally has them ready.

Oh, Molly, Molly, is it for this you came into the world, twice to give yourself without love? What difference does it make that your arms are strong and white if they can't clasp him to the softness and fragrance of your breast? Why are your eyes blue pools of love if they are not for his questioning and what are your rose lips for if they quench not his thirst?

Yes, I know God is very tender with a woman and I think He understands, so if she crept very close to Him and caught at His sleeve to steady herself He would

What are your rose lips for

be kind to her until she could go on along her own steep way. Please, God, never let him find out, for it would hurt him to have hurt me!

LEAF EIGHT

MELTED

SOME days are like the miracle flowers that open in the garden from plants you didn't expect to bloom at all. I might have been born, lived and died without having this one come into my life, and now that I have had it I don't know how to write it, except in the crimson of blood, the blue of flame, the gold of glory—and a tinge of light green would well express the part I have played. But it is all over at last and—

Ruth Chester was the unfolding of the first hour-petal and I got a glimpse of a heart of gold that I feel dumb with worship to think of. She's God's own good woman and He made her in one of His holy hours. I wish I could have borne her, or she me, and the tenderness of her arms was a sacrament. We two women just stood aside with life's artifices and concealments and let our own hearts do the talking.

She said she had come because she felt that if she talked with me I might be better able to understand Alfred when he came and that she had seen that the judge was very determined, and she thoroughly recognized his force of character. We stopped there while I gave her the document to read. I suppose it was dishonorable, but I needed her protection from it. I'm glad she had the strength of mind to walk with a head high in the air to Judy's range and burn it up. Anything might have happened if she hadn't. And even now I feel that only my marriage vows will close up the case for the judge—even yet he may— But when Ruth had got done with Alfred, she had wiped Judge Wade's appreciation of him completely off my mind and destroyed it in tender words that burned us both worse than Judy's fire burned the letter. She did me an awfully good service.

"And so you see, you lovely woman you, do you not, that God has made you for him as a tribute to his greatness and it is given to you to fulfil a destiny?" She was so beautiful as she said it that I had to turn my eyes away, but I felt as I did when those awful *'let-not-man-put-asunder'*—from Mr. Carter—words were spoken over me by Mr. Raines, the Methodist minister. It made me wild, and before I knew it I had poured out the whole truth to her in a perfect cataract of words. The truth always acts on women as some hitherto untried drug, and you can never tell what the reaction is going to be. In this case I was stricken dumb and found it hard to see.

"Oh, dear heart," she exclaimed as she reached out and drew me into her lovely gracious arms, "then the privilege is all the more wonderful for you, as you make some sacrifice to complete his life. Having suffered this, you will be all the greater woman to understand him. I accept my own sorrow at his hands willingly, as it gives me the larger sympathy for his work, though he will no longer need my personal encouragement as he has for years. In the light of his love this lesser feeling for Doctor Moore will soon pass away and the accord between you will be complete." This was more than I could stand and feeling less than a worm, I turned my face into her breast and wailed. Now who would have thought that girl could dance as she did?

By this time I was in such a solution of grief that I would soon have had to be sopped up with a sponge if Pet hadn't run in bubbling over like a lovely, white, linen-clad glass of Rhine wine and seltzer. Happiness has a habit of not even acknowledging the presence of grief and Pet didn't seem to see our red noses, crushed draperies and generally damp atmosphere.

"Molly," she said with a deliciously young giggle, "Tom says for you to send him ten dollars to spend getting the brass band half drunk before the six o'clock train, on which your Mr. Bennett comes. He has spent five dollars paying the negroes to polish up their instruments and clean up the uniforms and it cost him twenty-five to bail the cornettist out of jail for roost robbing, and it takes a whole gallon of whisky to get any spirit into the drummer. He says tell you that as this is your shindig you ought at least to pay the piper. Hurry up, he's waiting for me, and here's the kiss he told me to put on your left ear!"

"I suppose you delivered that kiss straight from where he gave it to you, Pettie, dear," I had the spirit to say as I went over to the desk for my pocket-book.

"Why, Molly, you know me better than that!" she exclaimed from behind a perfect rose cloud of blushes.

"I know Tom better than I do you," I answered as she fled with the ten in her hand. I looked at Ruth Chester and we both laughed. It is true that a broader sympathy is one of the by-products of sorrow, and a week ago I might have resented Pet to a marked degree instead of giving her the ten dollars and a blessing.

"I'm going quick, Molly, with that laugh between us," Ruth said as she rose and took me into her arms again for just half a second, and before I could stop her, she was gone.

She met Billy toiling up the front step with a long piece of rusty iron gas-pipe, which took off an inch of paint as it bumped against the edge of the porch. She bent down and kissed the back of his neck, which theft was almost more than I could stand, and apparently more than Billy was prepared to accept.

"Go way, girl," he said in his rudest manner; "don't you see I'm busy?"

I met him in the front hall just in time to prevent a hopeless scar on my hardwood floor. He was hot, perspiring and panting, but full of triumph.

184

MELTED

"I found it, Molly, I found it!" he exclaimed as he let the heavy pipe drop almost on the bare pink toes. "You can git a hammer and pound the end sharp and bend it so no whale we ketch can git away for nothing. You and Doc kin put it in your trunk 'cause it's too long for mine, and I can carry Doc's shirts and things in mine. Git the hammer quick and I'll help you fix it!" The pain in my breast was almost more than I could bear.

"Lover," I said as I knelt down by him in the dim old hall and put my arms around him as if to shield him from some blow I couldn't help being aimed at him, "you wouldn't mind much, would you, if just this time your Molly couldn't go with you? Your father is going to take good care of you and—and maybe bring you back to me some day."

"Why, Molly," he said, flaring his

astonished blue eyes at me, " 'taint me
to be took care of! I ain't a-going to
leave you here, for maybe a bear to come
out of a circus and eat you up, with me
and Doc gone. 'Sides Doc ain't no good
and maybe wouldn't help me hold the
rope right to keep the whale from gitting
away. He don't know how to do like I
tell him like you do."

"Try him, lover, and maybe he will—
will learn to—" I couldn't help the tears
that came to stop my words.

"Now you see, Molly, how you'd cry
with that kiss-spot gone," he said with
an amused, manly, little tenderness in his
voice that I had never heard before, and
he cuddled his lips against mine in almost
the only voluntary kiss he had given me
since I had got him into his ridiculous
little trousers under his blouses. "You
can have most a hundred kisses every

night if you don't say no more about not a-going and fix that whale hook for me quick," he coaxed against my cheek.

Oh, little lover, little lover, you didn't know what you were saying with your baby wisdom, and your rust-grimy, little paddie burned the sleep-place on my breast like a terrible white heat from which I was powerless to defend myself. You are mine, you are, you *are!* You are soul of my soul and heart of my heart and spirit of my spirit and—and you ought to have been flesh of my flesh!

I don't know how I managed to answer Mrs. Johnson's call from my front gate, but I sometimes think that women have a torture-proof clause in their constitutions.

She and Aunt Bettie had just come up the street from Aunt Bettie's house and the Pollard cook was following them with

a large basket, in which were packed the
things Aunt Bettie was contributing to
the entertainment of the distinguished
citizen. Mr. Johnson is Alfred's nearest
kinsman in Hillsboro, and, of course, he
is to be their guest while he is in town.

"He'll be feeding his eyes on Molly, so
he'll not even know he's eating my Washington almond pudding with Thomas' old
port in it," teased Aunt Bettie with a
laugh as I went across the street with
them.

"There's going to be a regular epi-
demic of love in Hillsboro, I do believe,"
she continued in her usual strain of senti-
mental speculation. "I saw Mr. Graves
talking to Delia Hawes in front of the
store an hour ago, as I came out from
looking at the blue chintz to match Pet
for the west wing, and they were both so
absorbed they didn't even see me. That

was what might have been called a conflagration dinner you gave the other
night, Molly, in more ways than one. I
wish a spark had set off Benton Wade
and Henrietta, too. Maybe it did, but is
just taking fire slowly."

I think it would be a good thing just
to let Aunt Bettie blindfold every unmar-
ried person in this town and marry them
to the first person they touch hands with.
It would be fun for her and then we could
have peace and apparently as much happiness as we are going to have anyway.
Mrs. Johnson seemed to be in somewhat
the same state of mind as I found myself.

"Humph," she said as we went up the
front steps, "I'll be glad when you are
married and settled, Molly Carter, so the
rest of this town can quiet down into
peace once more, and I sincerely hope
every woman under fifty in Hillsboro

who is already married will stay in that state until she reaches that age. But I do believe if the law marched widows from grave number one to altar number two they would get into trouble and fuss along the road. But come on in, both of you, and help me get this marriage feast ready, if I must! The day is going by on greased wheels and I can't let Mr. Johnson's crotchets be neglected, Al Bennett or no Al Bennett!"

And from then on for hours and hours I was strapped to a torture wheel that turned and turned, minute after minute, as it ground spice and sugar and bridal meats and me relentlessly into a great suffering pulp. Could I ever in all my life have hungered for food and been able to get it past the lump in my throat that grew larger with the seconds? And if Alfred's pudding tasted of the salt of dead sea-fruit this evening, it was from my surreptitious tears that dripped into it.

It was late, very late before Mrs. Johnson realized it and shooed me home to get ready to go to the train along with the brass band and all the other welcomes.

I hurried all I could, but for long minutes I stood in front of my mirror and questioned myself. Could this slow, pale, dead-eyed, slim, drooping girl be the rollicking child of a Molly who had looked out of that mirror at me one short week ago? Where were the wings on her heels, the glint in her curls, the laugh on her mouth and the devil in her eyes?

Slowly at last I lifted the blue muslin, twenty-three-inch waist shroud and let it slip over my head and fall slimly around me. I had fastened the neck button and was fumbling the next one into the buttonhole when I suddenly heard laughing excited voices coming up the side street that ran just under my west window. Something told me that Alfred had come on the five-down train instead of the six-up and I fairly reeled to the window and peeped through the shutters.

They were all in a laughing group around him, with Tom as master of ceremonies, and Ruth Chester was looking up into his face with an expression I am glad I can never forget. It killed all my regrets on the score of his future.

It took two good looks to take him all in and then I must have missed some of him, for all in all, he was so large that he stretched your eyes to behold him. He's grown seven feet tall, I don't know how many pounds he weighs and I don't want anybody ever to tell me!

I had never thought enough about evolution to know whether I believed in it and woman's suffrage, but I do now! I know that millions of years ago a great, big, distinguished hippopotamus stepped out of the woods and frightened one of my foremothers so that she turned tail and fled through a thicket that almost tore her limb from limb, right into the arms of her own mate. That's what I did! I caught that blue satin belt together with one hand and ran through my garden right over a bed of savage tiger-lilies and flung myself into John Moore's office, slammed the door and backed up against it.

"He's come!" I gasped. "And I'm frightened to death, with nobody but you to run to. Hide me quick! He's fat and I *hate* him!" I was that deadly cold you can get when fear runs into your very marrow and congeals the blood in your arteries. "Quick, quick!" I panted.

He must have been as pale as I was, and for an eternity of a second he looked at me, then suddenly heaven shone from his eyes and he opened his arms to me with just one word.

"Here?"

I went.

He held me gently for a half-second, and then with a sob which I felt rather than heard, he crushed me to him and stopped my breath with his lips on mine. I understood things then that I never had before, and I felt that wise guardian man-angel take his fingers from mine and leave me safe at last. I raised my hand and pressed it against John's wet lashes until he could let me speak and I was melted into his very breast itself.

"Molly," he said when enough tender-ness had come back into his arms to let me breathe, "you have almost killed me!"

"You!" I exclaimed, crowding still closer, or at least trying to. "It's not *you;* it's I that am killed, and you did it! I know you don't really want me, but I can't help that. I'd rather you'd do the suffering with me than to do it myself away from you. I'm so hungry and thirsty for you that—that I can't diet any longer!" I put the case the strongest way I knew how and got a swooning, maddening, luscious result.

"Want you, Molly?" he almost sobbed, and I felt his heart pounding hard next to my shoulder.

"Yes, want me!" I answered with more spirit than breath left in me. "I refuse to believe you are as stupid as I am, and anybody with even an ordinary amount of brains must have seen how hard I was fighting for you. I feel sure I left no stone unturned. Some of them I can already think back and see myself tugging at, and it makes me hot all over. I'm foolish, and always was, so I'm to be excused for acting that awful way, but you are to blame for *letting* me do it. I'm going to be your punishment for life for not having been stern and stopped me. You had better stop me some now anyway, for if I go on loving you as I have been for the last few minutes it will make you uncomfortable."

"Peaches," he said, after he had hushed me with another broken dose of love, as large as he thought I could stand—I could have stood more!—"I am never going to tell you how long I have loved you, but that day you came to me all in a flutter with Al Bennett's letter in your hand it is going to take you a lifetime to settle for. You were mine—and Bill's! How *could* you—but women don't under-

stand!" I felt him shudder in my arms
as I held him close. I was repaid for all
those tiresome exercises I had taken by
the strength to crush him against my
breast almost as hard as he crushed me.
Our combined strength was terrific, dangerous to life and ribs, but—heavenly!

"Don't women know, John?" I managed to ask softly in memory of a like
question he had put to me across that
bread and jam with the rose a-listening
from the dark.

What brought me to consciousness was
his fumbling with the buttons at the waist
of that blue muslin relict of a sentiment.
I had fastened but one, and the lace had
got caught on his sleeve buttons.

"Please don't button me into his possession," I laughed under his chin. "I'm
still scared to death of him, and you
haven't hid me yet!"

"Molly," he asked, this time with a heaven-laugh, "where could you be more effectually hid from Al Bennett than in my arms?"

I spent ten minutes telling Billy what a hippopotamus really looks like as I put him to bed, but later, much as I should have liked to, I couldn't consume that horrible dinner, that I had helped prepare at the Johnsons, in the shelter of John's arms, and I had to face Alfred. Ruth Chester was there, and she faced him too.

A man that can't be happy with a woman who is willing to "fulfil his destiny" doesn't deserve to be.

Then we came over here, and John had the most beautiful time persuading Aunt Adeline how a good man like Mr. Carter would want his young widow to be taken care of by being married to a safe friend of his instead of being flighty and having folks wondering whom she would marry.

"You know yourself how hard a time a beautiful young widow has, Mrs. Henderson," he said in the tone of voice that always makes his patients glad to take his worst doses. He got his blessing and me—with a warning.

A lovely night wind is blowing across my garden and bringing me congratulations from all my flower family. Flowers are a part of love and the wooing of it, and they understand. I am waiting for the light to go out behind the tall trees over which the moon is stealthily sinking. He promised me to put it out right away, and I'm watching the glow that marks the place where my own two men creatures are going to rest, with my heart in full song.

He needs rest, he is so very tired and

worn. He confessed it as I stood on the step above him to-night, after he had taken his own good night from me out on the porch. When he explained to me how his agony over me for all these months had kept him walking the floor night after night, not knowing that I was waiting for the light to go out, I gave myself a sweetness that I am going to say a prayer for the last thing before I sleep. I took his head in my arms and pressed his cheek down against Billy's sleep-place on my breast over my heart and put my lips to that drake-tail kiss-spot that has tempted me for I won't say how long. Then I fled—and so did he!

I had about decided to burn this book, because I shan't need it any longer, for he says he and Billy and I are going to play so much golf and tennis that I shall keep as thin as he wants me to be without any more melting or freezing, or starving, but perhaps he would like to read the little red devil.   Do you suppose he would?

THE END